THE GRIFFIN'S FEATHER

BOOK I IN THE MOLLY STEVENS &

THE NINE REALMS SERIES

THE GRIFFIN'S FEATHER

by Anne Harrington

Rothco Press • Los Angeles, California

Published by
Rothco Press
5500 Hollywood Blvd., 3rd Floor
Los Angeles, CA 90028
Copyright © 2014 by Anne Harrington

Cover design by Rob Cohen

Cover image by Adonna Khare

Rothco Press is a division of Over Easy Media Inc.

ISBN: 978-1-941519-10-3

Electronic ISBN: 978-1-941519-08-0

To Paris, Keegan, Ilias, Rowan and Tristan, for being my inspiration to write this book.

To my darling husband Mark, for being my reason for finishing it.

And, finally, to everyone who believed in Molly enough to keep me going when I was ready to quit.

-- Anne Harrington

CHAPTER 1

Molly Stevens stared out of the window and sighed. The sky was brown and reminded her of the inside of a dirty dishwater, although she wasn't exactly sure why. She brushed a finger down the window pane, hoping that the color was a film on the glass. But no, the air itself was dingy with dust and smog. Santa Geronimo was hot, dry and miserable—a far cry from the lush tropics of her home in Maui. It was definitely not what she'd envisioned when her mother told her they were moving to California. Instead of palm trees and beaches, there were just coyotes and tumbleweeds. Not a movie star for miles, unless she counted Boppo the clown, who made balloon animals at birthday parties.

She left the room and trotted downstairs. The rest of the house was no better, hot, stuffy and uncomfortably silent. Her mother was out doing errands with her younger brother, Dylan, in tow. Although she had been invited to go with them, Molly thought that staying home would be a better option than sitting in a hot car with a cranky toddler at the time, so she opted to stay home. Now she regretted that hasty decision. As she opened the front door she was hit with a hot breeze and felt herself break into a sweat under her light t-shirt. She groaned. If April was this miserable, she dreaded what August would be like.

She stepped outside. The stone felt nice and cool on her bare feet. Perched on the top step that descended from the porch, she squinted at the yellow grass in her front yard. Patches of dry, cracked earth punctuated the parched lawn every few feet, giving it a moth-eaten appearance. Looking across the deserted street at the other yards in similar shape, she frowned. "How can anyone stand this?" she asked no one in particular.

A slight movement on the edge of her line of vision caught her attention and she turned her gaze to the tangle of ivy under a thirsty-looking camellia bush. A lone, jet-colored bloom nodded in the hot breeze, as if beckoning her. *One of Mr. Cotton's black lilies!* She looked around, almost expecting the crazy old man to jump out from behind the shrub, glaring with his odd colorless eyes. Three months ago, when she and her family moved in, he marched up to them and explained that nobody was to touch anything from his garden, especially not those unusual flowers. *And why not?* Tons of them crowded his flowerbeds like an army of dark sentinels guarding his front yard.

As she approached, she took in the bloom. It seemed a little smaller than the others, as if by growing on her side of the fence it was somehow starved for something. *Water, probably.* Her mother was very strict with turning on the sprinklers. "Well," she addressed the flower, "Mom won't mind if you're a little runt of a thing. You'll still look nice in her bud vase." But the skin on the back of her arms prickled with alarm. *You know you're stealing...* her conscience objected. She hesitated for a split second. "No I'm not," she argued back. "It's growing on our side of the yard. Besides, it's only one and Mr. Cotton won't even notice. That stingy old man has lots of flowers."

Scanning the area for witnesses, she hurried over to the flower and kneeled. Now that she was close, she noticed that the black lily was unlike anything she'd ever seen. It was trumpet-shaped like a calla lily but where callas were smooth, this bloom was covered in tiny purple hairs. A large red stamen protruded like some kind of alien tongue from deep inside the flower's throat. Powdery pollen covered it, giving it a velvety look. About the same time she noticed these details, her mind registered a faint subtle perfume issuing from the lily. She couldn't put a name to the scent, but she thought it was what midnight might smell like if it had an aroma.

Taking a deep breath she grabbed the bloom, intending to break it off at the base of the stem. But rather than breaking cleanly, it disintegrated into a sticky mess in her hand. "Eeewwww," she exclaimed, momentarily forgetting that she was in stealth mode. She wiped the dark purple goo on the leg of her pants and contemplated whether to go grab another flower from her neighbor's yard. *Now that would really would be stealing,* she decided. She looked down at the ruined stem, weighing the potential risk of a daring daylight robbery versus bringing her mother such a wondrous present. One of her ears began to itch and she absent-mindedly dug a finger into it, scratching…

Stinging pain ripped through her, causing her eyes to tear up. She pulled her hand away and looked at her fingers, realizing that she had just rubbed flower juice into her ear. Suddenly Mr. Cotton's warning took on a whole new meaning. *Oh no! What if it's poisonous?* Panicking, she looked around for help. The solitude that she welcomed only minutes ago was now working against her. Her mom wouldn't be home for hours and she didn't know any of the other neighbors… except…

Molly heard a familiar creak as the door opened on the other side of the fence. "Who's out there?" a raspy voice called out. It was Mr. Cotton.

Fear gripped her. *He can't find out that I picked one of his flowers. Otherwise…* Visions of what he might do to her flooded her imagination, ranging in severity from prison to being boiled in a cauldron of purple lily juice. The stinging settled into a strange buzzing tickle as if a bumblebee was stuck in her ear canal. She almost stuck a finger in to relieve the sensation but then caught herself. *That's what got me in trouble in the first place,* she admonished herself.

Rising to her feet, she tried to ignore the dizziness that threatened to overtake her. "I'm dying," she groaned.

This time you've really messed up. You're going to have to tell Mr. Cotton what you've done.

"No," she argued with herself. "Not him. Anyone but him."

You have no choice. There's nobody else around and mama won't be home for hours. Anyway, they're his flowers. He's probably got an antidote or something.

She wobbled around the fence that separated their property. The buzzing faded to a tickle, but there was something wrong with the hearing in her left ear. Everything sounded like it was underwater and she could have sworn she heard the drone of a hundred voices whispering all at once. As she started up Mr. Cotton's driveway, his nasty little dog began to bark at her. But while she could hear it barking in her right ear, she heard something completely different in the other one:

"Barnaby, you old coot! That girl-creature is walking up to our house!"

Molly stopped in her tracks. She didn't remember the old man having a roommate, but she distinctly heard Mr. Cotton talking to somebody. "Good grief, Clarence. Settle down. I'm sure she doesn't mean any harm. She's probably just selling something," the old man said.

"Yeah right... And I'm a Leprechaun. That girl is trouble."

Molly stepped up onto the porch and rang the doorbell. Then, not knowing whether it actually worked or not, knocked on the door for good measure. "Hello? Mr. Cotton? It's me. Molly Stevens? From next door."

Her hearing was really messed up now. It sounded like the trees and bushes were muttering around her and she was almost sure she heard her name once or twice. Terror prickled the hair on the back of her neck and she rapped on the door again. "Please answer the door, Mr. Cotton. I know you're in there... and... I really need your help. It's an emergency!"

The door opened and Mr. Cotton's tall thin frame filled the doorway, looking both cross and puzzled. "What!?"

"Mr... C... C... C... Cotton?"

"Yes?"

She trembled and opened her mouth to speak, but nothing came out.

He scowled. "Well, what is it? No more cookies. I just bought two boxes of thin mints from the carrot top down the…"

"Ummm… I'm not a girl scout; I don't sell cookies."

He crossed his arms and peered down at her. His eyes gave off an odd glow, like a cat's in dim light. "Hmmph. I thought little girls always had cookies… Well, what do you want then?"

"Please," she whimpered, "I think I poisoned myself and I'm going to die." Tears streamed down her cheeks.

"I'm not a doctor. Go home and call 911." He shrugged and started to close the door.

"But Mr. Cotton! You gotta help me," she wailed. "I… picked one of those black lilies and…"

The old man's face turned bright red with anger. "You picked one of my lilies?" he exclaimed. "What have I told you about messing around in my garden?"

"I wasn't in your garden, Mr. Cotton. Honest!"

"Then how?"

Before she could answer, a brown flash shot past him and slowed to become a small feisty dog, yapping and nipping at her ankles. "Barnaby! Send her away! Can't you see she's trouble?"

It took a moment for Molly to register where the voice was coming from and her mouth dropped open in surprise. "The dog. It's…"

"It's what?" Mr. Cotton looked at her like she was crazy.

"Talking," she squeaked. The sound hurt her ears and she felt off balance. "Ooooowwww," she moaned.

"Oh for the love of chasing cats, it doesn't matter how," the dog growled.

"Obviously she got into your flowers. Look at her fingers!"

Mr. Cotton reached forward with surprising speed and grabbed Molly's hand. He peered at her purple-stained fingertips and then let go with a sigh.

Her panic returned and she remembered why she was there in the first place. "I… I scratched my ear. I think I might have gotten some of the juice in it. Now it hurts really bad."

He ran a clawlike hand through his thinning grey hair. "Does it tingle?"

She nodded glumly. "The lilies…" she asked in a timid voice. "Are they poisonous?"

"In a matter of speaking," the old man answered.

Molly started to cry.

"No! Stop that," the dog whined. "I can't stand it. Barnaby, make her stop!"

Mr. Cotton looked incredibly uncomfortable before stepping away from the door and motioning Molly inside. "Stop blubbering, would you? You're not going to die. Come inside. I have some tea brewing and we'll get you fixed up. You will be fine in a few hours."

"Really?" She sniffed and rubbed the tears from her eyes with her purple fingers.

Suddenly the world went black.

CHAPTER 2

"Oh my God! I'm blind!" Molly screamed. Her eyes tingled and burned. She knew right away she had rubbed flower juice into them as well. Large tears rolled down her cheeks.

The old man caught her hand before she could rub her eyes further and guided her inside, where he deposited her on a slightly musty-smelling couch.

"Child, you must relax," he admonished her. "You've really done it this time, I'm afraid. Let me finish getting the tea." Soon a clamor of dishes indicated that the tea was being served elsewhere in the house. "Keep still," he called out from the other room. "Your sight will return in a few minutes…"

"…In a matter of speaking…" the dog finished with a chuckle.

"Clarence! That was unnecessary," Mr. Cotton snapped.

"What does he mean by 'in a matter of speaking'?" she whimpered, the shock of a talking dog all but forgotten. "I'll be able to see again, right?"

"Molly—That's your name, right? Just stay calm and sit still. It will only be another minute or so."

He was right. Slowly the darkness lifted and turned into grey smoke, which then separated into many colors. Blurry shapes sharpened into pieces of furniture and an assortment of bric-a-brac. Soon she saw quite clearly again. But something was different. The dog that shared the couch with her before was gone and something very strange had taken its place...

Molly gave a stifled scream and scrunched over as far as she could.

"Sounds to me like the cat's out of the bag," Mr. Cotton grumbled from the kitchen. "You can see him now, can't you?"

"Ummm... yeah, I guess" Molly replied slowly in order not to startle the thing sitting next to her. She was not quite sure what to make of it, as she had never seen anything like this before. The beast had the head, wings and talons of an impossibly large eagle and the torso, back legs and tail of a lion. Its fur and feathers were pitch black, except for its head and the tip of its tail, which were brilliant gold. Its head was pure eagle except for two pointed and tufted fox-like ears that were currently laid back against its head like an angry house cat. Its talons and beak were shining steel and looked quite lethal. Molly inched over even farther to her side of the couch until she was hugging the arm.

Mr. Cotton strode into the room bearing an overloaded tea tray. "I see you've become acquainted with my friend's true appearance," he motioned casually towards the hissing beast on the couch as he set the tray down on the coffee table in front of her. "Clarence, don't be rude," he cuffed it on the head. "She's a child, not some Griffin-eating troll."

The creature gave a barely perceptible nod and slowly lifted his ears, one at a time.

"I... I... I thought Clarence was a DOG!" Molly gasped. "What *is* that?"

Clarence flattened his ears again and glared down his beak at her. "I am obviously not a dog nor a '*that*', young lady. I am a *Griffin*," he sniffed with disdain.

"Now, now," The old man said in a soothing voice as he poured steaming tea into two mugs and a larger cup that looked like a soup tureen. "There's no need to get your feathers ruffled." He chuckled. "To be quite honest, my friend, your appearance can be something of a shock to someone who's never seen a magical creature before."

"But… a… a *dog*, Barnaby?" Clarence snapped back. "Of all the ridiculous animals…"

"Well, what else do you think non-magic folk see you as? A hamster, perhaps?"

The Griffin didn't answer. He turned away and examined his claws. Molly was not sure at first if he behaved more like a bird or more like a cat, but after a moment of watching him, finally decided on the latter. She didn't know much about eagles, but he acted in a haughty manner similar to every other cat she knew. Barnaby passed Molly a plain coffee mug filled with tea and motioned to the tray.

"Someone ate all of the thin mints" he said, giving Clarence a sideways look. "But I found some gingersnaps. You children like gingersnaps, right?"

Molly took her tea and looked at the small plate of dusty-looking cookies. "I'm really not hungry. But thank you for offering," she added quickly, remembering what her Nana always told her about addressing grownups.

Mr. Cotton passed the oversized cup to the Griffin, who accepted it by gingerly balancing it between his claws. "It's his special cup," the old man explained. The Griffin dipped the tip of his beak into the cup and lapped with a contented sigh.

"Sir?" Molly ventured. "I'm sorry I thought you were a dog, but you did look like one before…" She trailed off and looked uneasily at the Griffin. It suddenly hit her. "This is what you meant, isn't it?" she asked, pointing at her eyes.

Clarence looked at her and tilted his head just slightly in answer. "Sharp as a stump, this one," he muttered.

The old man started to explain. "Those lilies you picked from my garden are a rare and unusual subspecies of fairy lilies, called *Zephranthes occulanium*. But they're also known as vision lilies in the Faerie tongue."

"I told you, the flower was in my yard…" Molly interrupted.

"Wait, did you say 'fairy'?"

He sighed. "Yes, child, Faerie. The lilies come from their world and have a rather unique property." He pointed to her purple fingers. "When you tried to pick the lily, you inadvertently crushed the flower in your hand and rubbed the juice in your ear and eyes. Now you are experiencing the consequences."

"I can hear things… and see things… that other people can't?"

He nodded. "Magical creatures are hidden in our world through '*glamour*', which is kind of a magic disguise. You see, people don't really want to believe that scary things like Clarence here actually exist, so the magic shows them more human-friendly animals, like cats and ducks and horses…"

The Griffin snorted. "And dogs."

"…And dogs," Barnaby agreed. "But the lily blocks the effects of the glamour, which is why you can see and hear Clarence in his true form."

"But he was so small before. Now he's so… huge!"

Barnaby chuckled. "That is one of the properties of glamour. It's magic, so things like mass and space have different rules. A giant could take on the form of a mouse." He paused and a faraway look crossed his face. "Well, I guess theoretically he could. But most magic creatures have absolutely no say as to what their glamourized form is. As far as I can tell, most of them don't even know what they look like to non-magic folk, let alone control it."

Clarence rolled his enormous green eyes and shook his head at Barnaby. "I knew growing those lilies was a bad idea. Now look what's happened," he reprimanded the old man and pointed a talon at Molly. "What are we going to do with her?"

"I don't know," Barnaby answered solemnly. "She knows our secret now. There's no going back." He took a sip of tea and set down his cup. A queer twinkle danced in his eyes. "But I think I have a perfect punishment that will be fitting for her crime."

The Griffin looked alarmed. "She knows too much. Let's feed her to the basilisk. Then she won't be a problem."

Barnaby scowled. "No my friend. We are not in the habit of feeding little girls to our guests. Even ones who don't follow directions and steal flowers."

"Like I said before, I didn't steal the flower," Molly objected. "Anyway, I just wanted it for mama."

"Oh, that changes everything now, doesn't it?" Clarence growled at her. "If indeed you are telling the truth, which I doubt." He turned back to Mr. Cotton. "We have to do something with her before she blows our cover. The basilisk will devour every last bit of her, even the bones. There won't be anything left."

Molly gulped.

The old man scowled at him. "We are not going to harm the girl and that's final."

"But what if she talks?" the Griffin whined.

"My friend, you watch a little too much TV. We're not fugitives from the law." Barnaby turned to Molly. "You can be trusted to keep a secret, can't you, child?"

She nodded vigorously. She wasn't quite sure what a basilisk was, but she was certain that she didn't want to be its next meal.

The old man continued. "What happened to you today has to be kept a secret. You can't tell anyone what happened here or what you've seen. Otherwise people will think you're crazy and take you away from your parents. And you must never again pick the vision lilies. Can you promise me this?"

Molly nodded. She couldn't imagine what life would be like without her mother and little brother. "I promise. But how long will I be able to see and hear... *him*?" she asked, motioning at Clarence.

The Griffin laid his ears flat against his head and looked insulted.

"I'm not exactly sure how long the effect will be on you. It may be a few hours or a few days," Barnaby answered slowly. "It's different for everyone."

Molly bit her lip so that the old man and his strange pet wouldn't see her smile. The idea of being able to see and hear magic was the most fantastic thing she'd ever imagined. It was like something out of a storybook.

He continued. "As for your punishment... For the crime of picking the lily, you will come here after school and help me feed and clean out the cages of my guests all next week. I will explain the situation to your mother."

"No, please don't tell her! She works late every day so she doesn't need to know!"

"Now, you know I can't do that. That would be extremely irresponsible of me not to let her know where you are. But I'll explain that you are simply 'helping' me so that she doesn't need to know you've gotten yourself in trouble, okay?"

She relaxed. "Thanks, Mr. Cotton."

Clarence made a strangled sound in the back of his throat and glared at Barnaby. The old man turned his back on the Griffin and focused his full attention on the girl. "Okay. You start tomorrow. Now remember, you need to follow every direction down to the letter. Do you understand?"

"Yes, of course! I promise to do everything you tell me," Molly squealed with delight. Then she frowned. "But what if the juice wears off? Can I have more?"

"Absolutely not. When it wears off you will still see the creatures, just not their more... *exciting* forms. You can still help out."

"Exciting? That's a bit of an understatement," Clarence rumbled.

Molly ignored the Griffin's snide remark. "Yes sir," she said, saluting Barnaby. "And I promise not to ever pick those flowers again," she added for good measure.

The Griffin narrowed his eyes and lowered his great feathered head until it was inches from Molly's. "You must swear upon the life of your mother that you will not breathe a word of what you've seen tonight to anyone—not your siblings, not your mother—not even your *bestest girlfriend*," he said with a sarcastic note on the last two words. "Or else there will be nasty consequences." He lifted one great talon and flicked out his claws one by one for effect.

She shivered and squeaked, "Yes sir!"

He stared at her with his emerald green eyes for a long time. Molly felt as if he was drilling down into her soul and examining it thoroughly for flaws. Finally he released her from his gaze.

"I will hold you to your word." He pricked up his ears and listened for a moment. "You should go now. I'm sure you have homework."

"Oh my gosh!" she exclaimed. "I totally forgot!" She carefully set her empty mug back on the tea tray, noticing that the cup handle now sported a set of purple fingerprints. "Sorry about that."

"You should wash your hands before you go. No use getting in any more trouble," Clarence observed.

"Right," Molly agreed and followed Barnaby to the kitchen. She washed her hands in the sink and started to wipe them on her pants.

Barnaby motioned towards the purple stains on the legs of her jeans. "That's a bad habit, you've got there," he commented as he handed her a damp hand towel.

Molly looked down at her jeans as she dried her hands. "I'll be more careful from now on." She handed him back the towel and rushed to the front door. "Goodbye, Mr. Cotton and thanks!"

CHAPTER 3

The next day, Molly hurried home from school. Mr. Cotton was on the front porch organizing a stack of empty animal carriers. Clarence dozed off to one side, his great golden head tucked under an inky black wing. He opened one eye slightly at the sound of her approach and sneezed.

"Bless you," Molly said.

"I see the juice hasn't worn off yet," he growled.

She grinned. "I guess it hasn't. I wasn't sure since I haven't seen anything... well... you know... *weird*... all day. Except for Peter Johnson, but he's just weird anyway. Nothing magic about him."

Clarence snorted and tucked his head back under his wing. Molly stepped up onto the porch, carefully avoiding the Griffin's tail, which was flicking this way and that.

"Hi, Mr. Cotton!"

Barnaby jumped, almost dropping a carrier that he had been trying to perch on top of a growing tower.

"Oh hi, Molly. I was just wondering when you'd come by. And here you are." His usually grumpy expression had softened into something almost friendly. She thought he might actually be glad to see her.

"Well I promised to come and I don't break my promises. Besides, mom said I should help out whenever I can." She didn't want him to know the truth—that she couldn't wait to come over and see the rest of Mr. Cotton's 'guests' and that she was so excited that she hadn't slept the night before.

He set down the carrier and motioned towards the open door. "Now that you're here we can go on back."

She stopped before going inside. "Can I ask you a question? How do you see the magic animals? Are you magic?"

"That's two questions..." Clarence groaned as he rose to his feet.

Mr. Cotton chuckled as he held the door open for the Griffin. "Me? Magic? Of course not! I rely on the lilies the same way you do."

Molly remembered the stinging pain and shuddered. "You willingly put that stuff in your eyes?"

"Well, of course," the old man replied. "Every morning when I wake up. Being able to see magical creatures is part of my job."

"I thought my mom said you were some kind of dog catcher or something." She pointed at the battered pickup in the driveway. "Your truck says 'Animal Protection Agency' on it."

"Well, no," he admitted, looking embarrassed. "I'm not exactly affiliated with the APA. The truck is a cover. It allows me to work in peace without having to explain myself. I do rescue animals, but it's not what most people expect. You see, I find magical animals that have gotten stuck here in this world for one reason or another."

Clarence interjected. "We can't really drive around town in a convertible with wild animals or livestock in the backseat. People ask questions, want to see licenses... The whole business can be one messy bureaucratic nightmare."

Molly wondered exactly how much experience a Griffin would really have with city bureaucracies—or licenses. "I guess it makes perfect sense when you think about it," she decided. "What do you do with the animals once you rescue them?"

Barnaby answered. "Well, usually I bring them here as my guests, in case they need some care. Most do, you know." His face flushed with anger. "Magical creatures seem to end up in the most miserable conditions. Starvation… physical abuse… you would be surprised at how badly some people treat their pets. But sometimes it's just a matter of reacquainting them with a world they may have forgotten."

"Huh?"

"Sometimes these poor animals have been away for so long that they completely forget who they are. They become dependent on their human masters. I can't exactly return them back to the magic realm in that condition—they wouldn't be able to take care of themselves." He moved towards the back of the living room, where dusty drapes obscured a set of French doors. "So I take them in and care for them until they're ready to go back." He threw back the curtains dramatically to reveal windows too dirty to see through. "Behold!"

"Wolfsbane and dragon breath!" Clarence swore and rolled his eyes in disgust. "Do you have to do that?"

"I guess it didn't quite have the effect I wanted," Barnaby said with a sheepish grin. "I really must remember to get those windows washed…" He opened one of the French doors.

Molly peered outside and thought at first she must be imagining things. There were acres and acres of rolling grasslands sporting wildflowers of every color imaginable. Several large barns stood in the distance. Beyond them she could just make out a large pond shimmering in the sunlight, bordered on three sides by a huge forest of magnificent trees that went on as far as her eyes could see. Everything was lush and green, a far cry from the ugly, dry landscape choked with dead brush and prickly tumbleweeds in her own backyard.

"H… how…" she stammered in shock.

"Well it's kind of hard to explain," Barnaby began. "It has to do with a lot of quantum mechanics, you know. Suffice to say, this is where the edge of the magic realm touches our world."

"Was it always like this?" Molly asked in awe.

"Oh, heavens no!" Barnaby explained. "When I first bought the house, the backyard was like every other yard in the neighborhood. One day I was clearing out a particularly thick tangle of blackberries at the far back of the yard and ran across a stray clump of vision lilies. Like you, I discovered their powers quite by accident." He pointed to a spot about fifty feet from the house, where a white fence cut across the grass. "See that fence? That's where this world ends," he said. "The rest of it—well you wouldn't see it without the lilies."

"It's beautiful," Molly sighed. "When do I get to explore it?"

"You won't. I don't know how much longer you'll be able to see the magic world, so it's better not to take any chances." The old man pointed to a shed about ten feet away from the house. "You're going to help me in there, with some of my smaller guests."

"Ummmmm… Where's the basilisk?"

Behind her, Clarence sniggered.

"Oh him? Well, we keep him in the shed. You'll meet him in a few minutes. He's nocturnal though, so he's not much of a conversationalist until the sun goes down."

Molly thought back to the night before. Instead of focusing on her math homework, she had gone through her collection of fantasy books until she found a description of a basilisk. According to the book it was huge and definitely ate children. Yet Mr. Cotton had said the shed was for 'smaller guests' and planned to take her to meet the creature. *The book's probably wrong*, she decided. "Do you have to speak basilisk to talk to it?"

Her question incited another snicker from the Griffin.

"Most magic creatures who have been in this world for more than a few weeks have picked up our speech and can communicate with us," Mr. Cotton explained. "The basilisk is one of these. However, some creatures can't make the sounds required for our language and so communication is difficult. Spanish seems to be a little better… I remember one time…"

"Ahem," Clarence broke in. "Barnaby, the sun sets early this time of year…"

"Ah yes, we must get started if I'm going to make introductions. I do hope you can see them long enough to meet them all. We're nowhere near full capacity but there are still a number of guests." He stepped outside and extended a hand.

Molly followed Mr. Cotton down the brick path to the shed. Clarence watched them for a moment and then turned back into the house. "Isn't he coming?"

"Him? Oh no. His favorite game show starts in a few minutes. He hasn't missed an episode in two years." The old man reached the door to the shed and produced a large keyring. Selecting a remarkably plain looking key, he unlocked the door and opened it.

The shed seemed much bigger on the inside than she expected. One side had a row of doors with barred windows, while the other was lined with cages. As soon as they entered, the room erupted with noisy chatter from the occupants.

"Hey, Barnaby, how's the weather?"

"Did you catch the game last night? Please tell me you did. That beastly flying monkey changed the channel right at the bottom of the ninth inning..."

"Who's the skirt?"

"Can I please have a little extra corn in my feed today?"

Barnaby traveled down the row, greeting each occupant and asking after their health and generally engaging in a touch of conversation. One by one, he introduced Molly to the creatures in his care. She shook the hands or claws of all who extended one to her and curtsied to the ones who didn't. Most of the creatures were friendly and polite, welcoming her and asking a few pointed questions, but nothing personal or embarrassing. She was surprised to see that the cages and stalls were open and the creatures had free access to roam around the shed if they wanted to. However, at the far end of the shed two stalls stood out, barred and locked with heavy padlocks. She pointed at them.

"What's in there?"

"Well, from time to time we get guests that can be dangerous. During their stay with us, we keep them locked up for their own safety as well as that of the others. The farthest stall is where the basilisk stays and the other one is housing a manticore cub." He moved to stand in front of the two doors. Molly peered in through the window of the closest one. A small cub slept in the far corner, its back towards the door and a large cast encasing one of its back legs. It looked exactly like a lion cub until it flicked its tail. Then Molly saw the cluster of barbed quills at the tip.

"Awwwww… He doesn't look so bad. I mean except for those spines."

"Don't be fooled. Manticores are carnivores—one of the few that prefer to hunt man. This little guy would just as soon tear your face off as look at you. And those spines are lethal. One scratch and you're good as gone. I've had to keep him sedated until his leg heals. Then he's going back to his pride."

"In the magic world?"

Barnaby shifted his weight uneasily. "Well, actually, no. He's too young to fend for himself and I just don't have the resources to attempt a relocation of a full pride of manticores back to the magic realm. So he's just going to have to go back to his family for now."

Molly turned from the cub's stall and stepped up to the next door. Barnaby grabbed her arm and pulled her away from the window. "Not so fast." He pointed at a pair of goggles hanging on a hook next to the stall. "You'll need to put those on first. The basilisk is quite gentle, but his gaze is instant death to all who make eye contact. It's truly an unfortunate condition. So I developed these goggles to shield my eyes when I tend to him."

"What happens? Does he turn people to stone?"

"Oh, no. He causes instant paralysis of the heart. If you looked at him without the goggles you'd drop dead where you stand."

"Shouldn't the goggles be on him?"

Barnaby laughed. "Well they wouldn't be much protection if you had to find a way to put the goggles on him. You'd be dead before you got within ten feet of him." He lowered the goggles over her eyes and strapped them in place. "These refract the basilisk's eyes just enough to render it harmless. It works on any creature with a lethal stare... basilisks... stony gazers..."

Molly looked around. The room seemed distorted, as if she was seeing everything through a glass of water. "Are you sure it's safe?"

"Absolutely. Try looking at him now."

She peered through the window at the top of the door and saw a small snakelike creature with tiny legs, not unlike a scaly salamander. But where a salamander only had four legs, this creature had eight. His head had a long snout, more like a crocodile or a dragon than a snake. "I was expecting him to be a lot bigger," she admitted. "Is he a baby?"

"No, he's pretty average-sized for his type. There are a few in East Asia that get a little bit bigger, but I don't think anyone's ever run across one that is more than about five feet long from snout to tail."

"Oh," She examined the creature again. He appeared black but as he moved, his scales reflected greens and blues. "He's really pretty."

The basilisk rose up until his front two pairs of legs were off the ground. He stared right at Molly with eyes that had an unusual purple-orange glow. She stepped back from the window, suddenly feeling slightly sick to her stomach.

Barnaby caught her arm and helped her down. "You saw his eyes, didn't you? I'm sure he didn't mean any harm—he probably just wanted to have a good look at you. He's a curious fellow. Still, it's a good thing you were wearing the goggles."

Molly nodded in agreement and handed them back to him. The queasy feeling immediately vanished. "What now?"

"Well, your first task will be to make sure this shed is cleaned up and that everyone here has fresh food and water." He pointed to a broom standing haphazardly in a corner, next to a bucket and a mop. "You can start with the flying monkey at the far end. Just whatever you do, don't give him any bananas, no matter how much he begs for them. He's horribly allergic—breaks out in the most awful boils."

Molly looked over at the cage that housed the creature in question. A purple ape sporting large bat-like wings grinned at her. "Gimmee banana," it squeaked. "Banana... banana... BANANA!"

Mr. Cotton shrugged. Then with a wave that almost looked like a salute, he left, shutting the door behind him. As soon as he was gone, a peanut shot by, narrowly missing her left ear.

She turned towards the flying monkey. "You heard what Mr. Cotton said. No bananas."

"Banana. Banana banana banana *banana!*" It lobbed another nut at her, this time hitting her squarely in the chest.

Molly sighed. It was going to be a long afternoon.

CHAPTER 4

Over the next several weeks, Molly spent every day after
school helping Mr. Cotton tend to the magical creatures
in his care. She worked hard and cheerfully did everything asked of her, even if it meant mucking out the stalls where
the winged horse and the unicorn were kept, or gathering fresh
earthworms for the giant toad or feeding the basilisk. As it turned
out, basilisks did not eat little girls—they preferred a diet of
cockroaches, slugs and snails. Barnaby said he would have liked to
keep him permanently in the garden, if there was any way to keep
the diminutive creature from killing the neighborhood cats with
his gaze.

Each day when Molly knocked on Barnaby's front door, she
made a silent wish that the door wouldn't be answered by a small
yapping dog. But much to her continued relief, the door was
opened by the large winged Griffin, who would peer at her for
a minute as if she were a stranger selling used toilet paper. His
greeting was always the same: "Good grief! You again?"

To which she always answered, "Of course it's me again, silly.
Who else would it be?" Then she would say something nice about
how polished his feathers looked or some other nice remark,
because her mother always said that grumpy people couldn't stay
grumpy if they were complimented enough.

Clarence usually just rolled his eyes dramatically and groaned.
"I guess this means it hasn't worn off yet, has it?" And then he
would let her inside.

The lingering effects of the lily were an ongoing topic of conversation. Molly wasn't sure if Mr. Cotton was excited or worried that it didn't seem to be wearing off. Some days he seemed a little anxious, other days he just shrugged his shoulders and remarked, "Everyone reacts differently, so what's the harm in it? I'm sure it will wear off eventually. It always does."

Molly secretly hoped the magic would never wear off. Her visits to Mr. Cotton's house were the highlight of an otherwise boring life. Now that her penance for her trespassing was long fulfilled, Mr. Cotton asked her to continue coming over to help as long as she still had the Sight so he could "...keep an eye on her." But once she ceased to be able to see or hear magic, the unspoken message was that there would be no reason for her to come over anymore. Life would go back to the dull drab existence she loathed before the day she tried to pick that black lily.

As time passed, even Clarence warmed up to her. As soon as their ritualistic greeting was over and she was inside, he would offer her some tea before peppering her with questions about all the marvels that made up such a large part of a modern pre-teenager's life: malls, the internet, smart phones, skaters, music videos, Twinkies, global warming, diet soda and any other topic that fancied him or he saw on television. Molly patiently answered every question, even if they sometimes were a little odd.

"Why do you put paint on your claws?" he asked her one afternoon.

"It's not paint, it's called nail polish."

"Why? It's not polish either."

"I don't know. That's just what its called," she replied a little defensively.

"Well they should call it nail *paint*. It looks like paint." He flicked his tail at her insolence. "But why do you put it on your claws? Barnaby doesn't."

"Of course not," she snickered. "He's an old man."

"Ah. So it's something only little girls do? Hmph." He narrowed his eyes and looked skeptical. "That can't be right. Do you remember that guy on the music video we watched yesterday? You know, the one dressed up like a ghoul? His claws were painted and he didn't look like a little girl to me…"

"It was part of his costume. For the video," Molly laughed. "Normally, guys don't wear nail polish. It's like…" she paused, trying to find a suitable comparison. "…like lipstick." She noticed his disappointed expression and tried to hide a smile. "Were you thinking of painting your claws?"

Clarence looked uncomfortable and shifted his position on the couch. "Nope. Never entered my mind. I just wanted to know why you do it," he shot back. "Anyway, don't you think it's about time you got to work, young lady?"

She left the room in search of Barnaby. When she was safely outside and out of earshot of the Griffin, she burst out laughing. The picture of Clarence with his scary-sharp talons painted bright pink was too much. She ran across the field peppered with tiny blue daisies and pink chamomile until she spotted the old man outside of the main barn. He looked a little sad today.

"Hiya, Mr. Cotton," Molly called out. "Are you okay?"

"Oh, hello, Molly. I'm fine. I just get a little teary when I say goodbye to one of my guests," he replied with a soft smile.

Molly nodded in understanding and felt a twinge of sadness. Marcus was a winged horse that Barnaby had rescued from a particularly bad situation. The old man found the magical creature at an auction house several months ago, disguised as a small goat and painfully thin. He had been horribly abused and wouldn't talk to anyone, even Mr. Cotton.

Molly brought Marcus carrots and apples every time she visited, and once in a while even snuck him his favorite treat—black licorice jellybeans. He quickly learned to trust her and soon started telling her the most wonderful stories about growing up in the rich pasturelands east of Shangri-La. He even let her ride on his back once or twice—although he promised Mr. Cotton that they wouldn't fly. Molly didn't mind; she was a little afraid of falling off, since she had never ridden bareback before.

Her equine friend's last molt revealed beautiful, healthy feathers, a shining coat of silver and a long white mane and tail that gleamed iridescently in the sun. It was a complete transformation from the drab grey, dead-looking animal Molly remembered from her first visit to the barn. But it also meant that Marcus was fully recovered and ready to go home. She always knew he would eventually leave—Mr. Cotton said all of his guests went home sooner or later—but it was a little sad to lose her first charge.

The old man continued. "He'll go into the Forest today. He would left sooner, but he wanted to say goodbye to you."

The 'Forest' was a nickname they called the buffer zone between Barnaby's backyard and the magic world. It was fitting, since the grove of trees at the edge of his property marked the path to the magical lands beyond. But even with the lily's magic, the realm itself was hidden from her.

"Why can't I see the magic world?" she had asked Mr. Cotton on her first trip to the barn.

"Because sometimes you can't see a forest for the trees," he answered.

And so the name 'Forest' had stuck.

A horse's whinny jolted Molly back to the present. The flying horse emerged from the barn and trotted up to her. He nudged her hard, looking for a treat. She pulled a handful of black jellybeans from her right front pocket. Barnaby scowled, but she didn't miss the twinkle in his eyes. She held out the candy to Marcus, who gobbled them up.

"Clarence did you both a big favor by telling you about Marcus's love for jellybeans," Barnaby observed.

"Actually, he didn't, Mr. Cotton. Marcus did."

Barnaby raised one eyebrow. "Curious… I always thought Marcus started talking to you because you brought him candy, not the other way around." He scratched his jaw thoughtfully. "You do seem to have a special way with my guests. I'm actually not surprised this one trusts you." He turned to the horse. "Well, it's time to go home, my friend. Are you ready?"

Marcus bent his neck until his nose was nuzzling Barnaby's ear.

"Of course she can come as far as the Forest," the old man replied. "But no farther."

Molly smiled as she stroked Marcus' shimmering mane. The trio went around to the far side of the barn and entered the grove through a rickety wooden gate. Grand old live oaks and fragrant eucalyptus trees soon gave way to more exotic species that she had never seen before. The air cooled and smelled fresh and alive, as if washed by a spring rain. Passing by a tree with an exceptionally smooth trunk, he stopped to knock on the trunk. She was surprised at the hollow metallic sound.

"Ironwood," he explained as he prodded her along. "Probably not a good idea to rest here. You never know when a branch will fall."

As they pressed deeper into the Forest, Molly became aware of a strange white fog that rolled in between the massive trees and obscured the path ahead of them. The farther they went in, the thicker the fog became, swirling around their feet and cloaking the ground. Barnaby stopped at a place where a log had fallen across the path. Beyond the log, the mist formed a solid wall that reached up to the sky and obscured everything. "My dear, this is where we must say goodbye," he said. "We can't go any farther."

She squinted, but couldn't make out even the shapes of the trees that she knew must be there, hidden in the mist. "Why can't I go into the fog? What's in there?" she asked.

Marcus looked at her curiously. "I don't understand. There's no fog," he nickered.

"There actually isn't any fog, Molly," Barnaby explained. "This is where the magical world starts. It remains hidden from you and I. The magic that keeps it concealed from us is stronger than the vision lilies. We won't ever be able to see it, I'm afraid."

The flying horse snorted and butted his head into Molly's shoulder. "Let's go. My herd is close by. I can smell them!"

"I'm sorry, Marcus. I can't go with you," she replied sadly. "You have to go on home and find your herd by yourself."

The winged horse tossed his head and stretched his magnificent wings. "I won't forget you, Molly. You and Barnaby showed me that there are good people even in this place. He nudged her. "Take a hair from my mane. If you need me, hold it and say my name three times. No matter where I am, I'll rush to your side." Molly carefully pulled a single hair and held it close. Then she gave him a hug around his neck and stepped away to give him room. He lept over the fallen tree and into the air, circling higher and higher, in and out of the trees. "Brothers, I return!" He wheeled around and circled back a final time, before disappearing into the mist.

Molly and Barnaby stood in silence for several minutes, staring in the direction Marcus had taken.

"It's always hard to let them go." The old man put a comforting hand on her shoulder as they began walking back the way they came. "At the same time it's a wonderful feeling knowing that we've helped another magical creature get home."

"Yeah." She looked at the horsehair in the palm of her hand. It sparkled in the mottled sunlight as if spun from a diamond. She carefully coiled it into a circlet and wove the ends into the loops.

"That's a very special gift," Mr. Cotton commented. "It wouldn't be good to carry it in your pocket. It might get lost. But I think I might have something back at the house that you can put it in to keep it safe."

There was another whinny from Marcus, far off in the distance. It was answered this time by two equine voices. Marcus had found his herd.

CHAPTER 5

Clarence was waiting for them on the back porch when they returned. He had an oddly perturbed expression. "Barnaby, you've got…"

Mr. Cotton waved him off with an impatient gesture. "Yes, Clarence. Whatever it is you need me to do right now can wait a minute. I've got to find that locket…" He trailed off as an unfamiliar figure stepped out of the door behind the Griffin.

"…Visitors," Clarence finished. He moved over to the far end of the porch to make room, coming to a stop right behind Molly.

Molly knew something was wrong by the way Mr. Cotton stopped short and bowed to the stranger. The woman gave an almost imperceivable nod in reply. She mostly looked human, but her long pointed ears and pale skin gave her away. *She must be an Elf*, Molly thought. But this creature was not like any picture of an Elf she'd ever seen. She didn't have any gossamer wings or gown made of butterfly silk. Instead her dark hair was pulled back into a tight bun and she wore a well tailored navy blue suit with a small badge pinned on her lapel. She didn't look magical at all. In fact, she resembled a cop…

The woman peered at her. "Very perceptive, for a human," she commented rather drily, as if making an observation about the weather, and turned her attention back to Mr. Cotton. She removed an identification badge from her pocket and flashed it at him. "Constable Taralinda. From the Magic Compliance

Committee. You are, of course aware of the reason for my visit today?"

Mr. Cotton blinked and shook his head. "No, I'm afraid not."

She shrugged. "Very well. There has been a report of a non-authorized use of occulanium potion on a human juvenile." She nodded towards Molly. "I'm assuming that is the child in question."

The color left Barnaby's face. "It wasn't a non-authorized use. I didn't give her any potion. She touched one of the flowers by accident."

Molly's mood soured. Magical or not, she didn't trust cops... or constables. Especially ones who knew what she was thinking. Plus, she hated when adults talked about her like she wasn't there when she was standing two feet from them.

Taralinda traced a square in the air at face height. A document materialized inside, hanging in midair as if attached to an unseen string. She snapped her fingers and a pair of reading glasses appeared, balanced on her beaklike nose. "It says here that the incident happened over a month ago," she observed, pausing on a page covered in strange glowing handwriting. Peering over the glasses, she looked suspiciously at Barnaby. "So if this was indeed an accident, as you claim, why didn't you ever report it to the Committee? We could have removed the girl's Sight and put an end to her ordeal..."

"It's not an ordeal!" Molly interrupted. "And it's not his fault! I picked the flower and went to Mr. Cotton for help."

Taralinda ignored her outburst and continued reading from the report. "...It also states here that you allowed the human to interact with the animals under your care?" She clucked and wagged a finger at him. "Now you know perfectly well that Article 6203, Paragraph 47, section B, sub-section 37J clearly prohibits *contamination*..."

Molly looked at her fingers. Contamination? She opened her mouth again to object when a hiss in her left ear stopped her.

"Shhhhh. You need to be quiet. You're just making things worse for all of us," Clarence whispered.

Molly bit her lip and tried not to say anything. Inside she was seething. Mr. Cotton was so kind to all of the magic creatures—even the manticore. She wanted to tell the constable that he would never put any of his guests in danger.

"…Of magic creatures from humans while in recovery," the constable continued. "I might have to shut down this entire facility and revoke your license."

"Look, I was just trying to keep an eye on the child until the juice wore off. I figured it would only last a few days, maybe a week at most. I didn't contact you because I thought it would be a lot of trouble. Molly's a good kid and to be quite honest, she's been really helpful around here. I'm not as young as I used to be."

The Elf turned another page. Her eyes narrowed. "According to this you had a winged horse in your care?"

"Yes. We actually released him right before you arrived."

"You took the girl into the Magic Lands?"

"Oh no, of course not. We stopped before the border. I took her only as far as the Sight would allow."

The Elf relaxed and continued reading. "Well according to this, the girl is partially responsible for the animal's speedy recovery. And since there are no official complaints of damages arising from the incident…" Her thin lips curled into a hint of a smile. "…The recommendation I will put into my report is that you continue to monitor the girl at your facility until the magic wears off."

Barnaby sighed with relief. "Thank you."

"But once the child stops seeing magic, she must go back to her normal life. No more visits and *absolutely* no more lily juice. Accident or not, if this happens again, Mr. Cotton, I will have no choice but to take action against you."

"Yes, constable, I understand."

Her expression softened. "Listen Mr. Cotton, I was assigned to your case after my predecessor retired. You're a good man with a big heart and you've never caused me a spot of trouble in a hundred and thirty-six years. The last thing I want to ever see happen is this place close down. So I'm going to give you a second chance."

Molly's jaw dropped, but before she could say anything Clarence hissed in her ear again. "Don't ask."

Removing her glasses, Constable Taralinda made a quick motion with her thumb and forefinger. The floating document and the spectacles both vanished. "Don't disappoint me. If this happens again I will have no choice but to revoke your license and shut this place down." With that she vanished with a pop that sounded like a soap bubble bursting.

Clarence got up and took her place. "Well kids, that was entertaining," he yawned. "I think after all of that excitement I'm going to go take a nap." He disappeared into the house. Despite his nonchalant manner, Molly couldn't help but notice the nervous twitch in his tail. The visit from the constable had truly unnerved the great beast.

Mr. Cotton sank into a weatherbeaten patio chair. "That was close." He looked over at her. "Constable Taralinda really went out on a limb for us. I hope you realize this."

"I thought she was awful," she replied. "To threaten to close you down because of one little accident that wasn't even your fault."

"Yes, it's unfortunate, but often our actions harm those around us," Barnaby sighed. "But she really did us a favor. You see, by permitting me to watch over you, she is really letting you stay and help me."

Molly looked down at her feet. "I guess," she moaned. "But only until the magic wears off. After that I have to go back to my plain old boring life."

He smiled. "I guess all we can do is hope the magic is permanent. You never know where magic is concerned—maybe in your case it will stay. It's been well over a month with no signs of it going away. That's unheard of."

She nodded and looked up at the sky. The sun had set and she saw the twinkle of the first star of the evening. She made a silent wish to it, hoping that he was right.

CHAPTER 6

When Molly woke up the next morning and looked out of her window, she knew it was going to be a rotten day. The sky was overcast, but not enough to promise rain. Although it was almost summer, it was unexpectedly cold and grey. She grumbled and went to shut off her alarm, but misjudged the distance and instead knocked it off the nightstand with her elbow. The commotion woke her little brother, who started to howl.

"Dylan… Dylan… Shhhh… Please be quiet!" she begged. The last thing she wanted was for the toddler to wake their mother. But the more she tried to reason with him, the louder he yelled.

"Noodles!" he screamed. "I want noodles!"

"Noodles? We don't have any noodles. Besides, you can't have noodles for breakfast. It's just flat out wrong. How about cereal?"

"NOODLES!!!!" he screamed again.

She tried a different approach. "What if I made you a scrambled egg?"

His expression immediately changed and he squealed with joy. "I wanna egg!"

Molly sighed. Although she succeeded in quieting down her little brother, now she was stuck making him breakfast. Throwing on a slightly wrinkled T-shirt and a pair of blue jeans, she trudged downstairs into the kitchen. Dylan trailed behind, chattering about his favorite cartoon character. She opened the refrigerator, only to find that they were out of eggs. This sent the toddler into hysterics again. With a groan, she raided her secret stash of leftover Easter candy. She sat Dylan down in front of the television and gave him a handful of foil wrapped chocolates. "Here are some special eggs. Have a nice sugar rush," she said as she switched on a cartoon featuring a couple of animals beating each other up with mallets. She heard creaking upstairs and knew her brother's outburst had woken her mother, who would be down in another minute. It was time to make a speedy exit before her breakfast choice was discovered. The last thing she needed was a lecture on the evils of giving little brothers candy first thing in the morning. Already he was starting to bounce up and down on the couch, his mouth smeared with chocolate.

Molly stepped out onto the porch and shivered. In her haste to get out of the house she had completely forgotten about the weather. She toyed with the idea of going back inside to grab a sweater, but she knew Dylan would demand something else and make her even later than she was already going to be. She looked at the sky and decided to take her chances. It didn't look like it was actually going to rain, so she probably only had the morning chill to contend with. The clouds usually burnt off by lunchtime.

As she trudged past Barnaby's house she caught a glimpse of something shimmering out of the corner of her eye. An impossibly large shiny black feather had blown down his driveway and was now lodged between her fence and a thorny-looking Euphorbia bush. She recognized it immediately—it was a flight feather from one of Clarence's enormous wings. Smiling, she stooped and gingerly retrieved it, careful not to get poked by thorns in the process. It would be a great good-luck charm for when she was having a bad day at school. She was sure Clarence wouldn't mind. Besides, her classmates couldn't see the feather anyway, so it would be safe. She stroked the feather, admiring for a moment the way it shown iridescently. Then she opened her backpack and tucked it safely inside her binder.

She looked at her watch and groaned. She was going to be

late and there was nothing she could do about it. Her teacher, Mr. Richardson, was usually pretty good-natured, but only two days ago he had warned her that she absolutely could not be late again or he was going to start marking her tardy. She zipped up her pack and started running down the sidewalk towards the school.

Had she been in less of a rush, she might have noticed the creature sitting on the wall across the street. To any bystander, it appeared to be a smallish tabby cat with a funny crooked tail, but if Molly had glanced in its direction she would have seen it for what it really was: a greasy black hobgoblin wearing a pair of dirty white sneakers. It watched her open her backpack with the intensity of a lion stalking a gazelle, eyes glued to the feather in her fingers. As soon as Molly zipped up her backpack and started running, it broke into a smile that could peel paint. With a snap of its greasy fingers, it vanished into thin air.

It took Molly exactly seven minutes and thirteen seconds to get to the fence that surrounded the school. As she approached the gate she thought for a moment that she was actually going to make it inside before the bell rang, but the loud buzzer sounded off when she was a few feet away from the door. Mrs. Peabody, the rabid teacher's aide assigned gatekeeper duties that day, spotted her and gave her a triumphant look. "LATE!" she barked and pointed to the office door. "Go get a tardy slip."

Molly grumbled. Usually she was able to slip through the gate unnoticed and therefore avoid being officially LATE. "Yeah, yeah, yeah," she muttered sarcastically. "Do not pass 'Go'. Do not collect $200.00…"

"What did you say?" the teacher's aide shrieked.

Molly grinned through clenched teeth. "Nothing, Mrs. Peabody," she said as sweetly as she could muster.

The aide looked suspiciously at Molly as if she was going to question her further; but then changed her mind and dismissed her with a wave of a pudgy hand. "Just fill out the form and get to class before your teacher marks you 'truant," she snipped.

"Fat chance," Molly said under her breath as she reached

the office and pulled the heavy steel door open. Mr. Richardson might mark her tardy this time, but there was no way he was mean enough to mark her truant for being five minutes late. She quickly filled out the pink slip, purposely ignoring the smirking receptionist.

All hopes of the day improving were dashed when Molly slowly opened the door to her classroom and saw an unfamiliar female figure standing at the head of the class with her back turned. She froze. *A substitute! Can this day get any worse?* She slipped into the closest chair as quietly as possible and slowly unzipped her backpack.

"*You*," the substitute's voice rang out. "In the back." She pointed at Molly and all twenty-seven students turned around in their chairs and stared. "Please come to the front of the room. There is an empty seat up here. I will also need your tardy slip."

Molly groaned as several of her classmates laughed. "Yes Mrs…" she looked at the blackboard where substitutes customarily wrote their names. "…Gorgon."

The classroom erupted into giggles.

"That's Miss *Gordon*," the substitute corrected her, without turning from the blackboard. "Now hurry up, before you disrupt my classroom any further."

Molly grabbed her backpack and moved to the front of the room. Her face flushed hot with embarrassment as she passed the rows of snickering students on either side. Then the unthinkable happened. In her haste, Molly forgot to zip her backpack all the way and it now opened, spilling the contents all over the floor with a loud clatter.

Miss Gordon whipped around at the sound and glared at Molly and the jumble of books and school supplies littering the floor. Her eyes narrowed. "Pick up that mess quickly and get to your desk," she barked.

Molly dutifully obeyed and slunk to her desk. *Great*, she thought. *Now I've made an enemy of the substitute.*

It was turning into one heck of a bad day.

CHAPTER 7

B y lunchtime, Molly was beginning to think that perhaps the day might turn out okay after all. After the morning's disruption, Miss Gordon ignored her and appeared to have completely forgotten about the tardy slip. There was a pop quiz that Molly managed to pass with a decent score, despite the fact that she had not quite finished the chapter. Her classmates seemed to collectively accept the backpack incident as enough torture for the day and thankfully left her alone. The morning passed faster than she expected and suddenly the loud buzzer announced lunch. She got up to leave.

"Just a minute, Molly," Miss Gordon said. "I would like to have a word with you before you leave."

The other students hurried from the room, whispering and murmuring among themselves. Molly fidgeted in her seat, contemplating what the substitute might have in store. None of them involved positive outcomes. When the last stragglers finally left, Miss Gordon came over to her seat. She wore a smile that would frighten small children.

"I believe we didn't really get off to a good start this morning," Miss Gordon purred. "I'd like to get to know you better. You remind me of my own little girl."

Molly didn't buy that for a moment. With her perfectly coiffed hair, long manicured nails and impeccably tailored suit of white silk, Miss Gordon didn't look like she had a single maternal bone in her body. If the substitute did have a kid, Molly figured it was locked up in an attic or had been long ago bundled off to relatives. "Umm… what do you want to know?" she asked nervously.

"Oh, I don't know," Miss Gordon replied, "what you like, what you don't like, where you live, what you like to do when you're not in school…" she smiled again, "…You know, *every-thing.*" She was trying to sound friendly but it wasn't working. There was a cold predatory gleam in her blue eyes.

Molly hesitated, mentally going over the pros and cons of telling Miss Gordon her life story. Finally she decided that telling her teacher an abridged version would be the best call. "I'm from Maui—that's in Hawaii," she began cautiously. "I've been here almost six months. I live with my mom and my little brother…" She paused, trying to find something else to say that wouldn't reveal too much. "I like animals and gardening." She almost kicked herself for saying the last point; it sounded like something on one of those dumb game shows.

"Oh, I love animals," Miss Gordon gushed a little too enthusiastically. "Especially birds. Bird watching is kind of a hobby of mine. Do you have many friends here at school?"

"No, not really," Molly replied, warming up to Miss Gordon's conversational tone. She realized how much she missed a teacher taking some kind of interest in her outside of how she did on tests. "But that's okay. I have other friends. Clarence always says…" She stopped herself, realizing she had almost made a fatal blunder.

"Clarence?" Miss Gordon looked at her curiously. "Is he a boy in your neighborhood?" She took off her glasses and peered at her.

Molly found herself entranced by her teacher's eyes. She thought they were blue at first but soon realized that they seemed to be changing color. She stared at them, trying to figure out if they were brown, green, hazel or turquoise — they were none of these colors and all of them at the same time. The more she stared the more she was not sure. "Clarence?" she murmured, so distracted by Miss Gordon's strange eyes that she forgot what she was saying. "Yeah, Clarence. He always says I don't need the silly kids at school."

Miss Gordon sat on the edge of Molly's desk, eyes locked onto Molly's. She repeated the question. "Clarence? Is he a boy you know?"

Molly shook her head. "He's not a boy…"

"…But he lives in your neighborhood," Miss Gordon finished the sentence. Her voice had a strange soothing quality to it, as if she were calming a small child.

Molly nodded, feeling calm and dreamy. "Yeah… next door. He lives with Mr. Cotton."

"And he was the one who gave you the feather."

"The feather?" Molly yawned.

"Yes, Molly," Miss Gordon replied softly. "In your backpack. I believe it's a Griffin's feather isn't it?"

Somewhere in the back of her mind Molly registered that her teacher wasn't supposed to know about Griffins or that she had a feather from one hidden in her backpack, but somehow it didn't seem very important at the moment. Her head felt very heavy and began to droop.

Miss Gordon reached out and gently caught Molly's head and cradled her chin, keeping the girl's gaze locked to her own. "The Griffin's feather, Molly. This is important. Where did you get it?"

"I found it," Molly mumbled. "It Clarence's."

"What's your address?"

"128 Maple Street."

Miss Gordon nodded thoughtfully and then an ugly cruel smile began to creep across her beautiful features. "Good girl. Now go to sleep."

Molly's eyelids drooped and she yawned again. She struggled against the weight of her eyelids as sleep overtook her. Just before dozing off, she thought she saw Miss Gordon whispering to a small ugly black creature wearing dirty white sneakers.

CHAPTER 8

Molly woke to the sensation of someone poking her. It was Tommy Woodbury, the boy who sat behind her. "Hey, geek! Wake up!" he laughed. "You slept through lunch!"

"Huh?" She tried to figure out how she fell asleep, but all that she could remember was the bell sounding for lunch and Miss Gordon asking her to stay for a minute to talk. The rest was a mishmash of wispy recollections that faded away before she could sort them out.

Just then the principal walked in with a mousy-looking woman trailing behind. All of the students stopped what they were doing and looked at the pair with expressions that ranged from alarm to curiosity. Everyone recognized the woman — she was also a substitute teacher. A few began to whisper excitedly, pondering the meaning of her presence.

"Attention students," he announced and strode to the front of the room. "There has been a slight change." He paused a moment to make sure that he had everyone's attention before continuing. "Your substitute, Miss Gordon, has had a family emergency and needed to leave. Mrs. Stone has graciously agreed to come in on short notice to teach the remainder of today's lessons."

Mrs. Stone was a familiar face around the campus and had taught their class more than once. She preferred to just set up a movie rather than actually teach anything. Students looked at each other and smiled. It was going to be a glorious afternoon.

The principal correctly interpreted the classroom reaction to mean that the students approved of the change, although he would have been appalled to know why. "All right, then. Unless anyone has any other questions, I will leave you here in the care of Mrs. Stone." He looked around for raised hands or confused students. Seeing none, he quickly left the classroom.

True to her anticipated behavior, Mrs. Stone immediately erased the blackboard of lessons, grabbed a DVD from her oversized bag, popped it into the video player and dimmed the lights. Then she pulled a laptop from the same bag and stuck in a wireless card. She plopped herself down at the desk and began her daily search for collectible figurines on eBay.

Molly yawned as the opening titles came up on the screen. The movie was a fairly dull, family-friendly comedy that she remembered from one of the substitute's previous visits. She didn't mind, as she was still really tired for some reason. She dozed through most of the movie.

The ending credits were just beginning to roll when the buzzer sounded the end of the school day. Molly got up and stretched. She was sore from falling asleep at her desk and her head ached. She wondered if Mr. Cotton had a magic potion that would work better than the generic store-brand children's aspirin her mother insisted on buying. *Better not to even think about that*, she concluded. The last thing she wanted was to get Mr. Cotton in trouble again over a headache remedy. She groaned, remembering that today her mother was picking her up from school to go grocery shopping. Between the wholesale food store, the discount pharmacy and the regular supermarket (to hunt down the things not found at the first two places) they would be gone for most of the afternoon. Although she was off the hook where homework was concerned, the errands meant Molly was not going to have much time today to spend with Clarence and Mr. Cotton.

Her mom was waiting at the curb in the battered family car. Molly grimaced when she saw the wreck and looked around, hoping none of her classmates were watching. The car was a '66 Mustang convertible, but not a cool restored classic. Instead of being a dreamy cherry red, it was a decidedly non-cool shade of baby blue, rusted and dented in places. The worn out seats smelled unpleasantly like cat spray on hot days. Molly referred to the car as 'The Beast' and swore she was going to run it off a cliff or send it into a lake just as soon as she had a learner's permit. Her mother, on the other hand, loved the car and insisted that once restored to its former glory, the car would be gorgeous. Molly yanked at the perpetually sticky passenger side door until it opened with a loud creak. She slid into the torn front seat without hesitation, noticing an assortment of bags in the back.

"Looks like you started without me," she frowned in mock disapproval. Inside she was relieved.

Her mom smiled. "Well, I had a little extra time, so I thought we would get some of the errands out of the way before picking you up."

Molly noticed bags from all of their usual haunts. "It looks like you took care of all of it," she smiled. "What's left?"

"Actually just the post office and then I thought we'd hit Burgerland," her mother replied. "They have a new chocolate chip peanut butter milkshake…"

"Mmmmmm… Sounds good. Can I go to Mr. Cotton's house when we get home?"

"Do you have a lot of homework?"

"Nope. We had a sub." It was almost the truth. Although Miss Gordon had given them copious amounts of reading, Molly figured Mrs. Stone trumped it when she erased the assignments from the blackboard. Anyway, it was highly unlikely Miss Gordon would return to check up on their homework. Molly shuddered as she recalled the strange substitute with the odd eyes. Just thinking about her gave Molly the chills. It was as if she was remembering part of a bad dream.

"Are you okay?" her mother asked. "The color just drained out of your face. You're not getting carsick, are you?"

"No, I'm fine," Molly lied. "Just a little hungry. I skipped lunch."

"You can see if there's something you can snack on in the back, if you want."

Molly reached behind her and rummaged around until she found a bunch of grapes in the top of one of the bags. She broke off a stem.

"Those haven't been washed," her mother warned.

Molly shrugged and popped one into her mouth. The sweetness washed over her tongue and she suddenly realized how famished she was. She quickly finished the bunch and reached around to get more.

"No more, young lady," her mother laughed. "You're going to ruin your appetite for burgers."

A sudden vision of Miss Gordon's strange eyes hit Molly again. She immediately felt cold and nauseous.

Her mother glanced over at her. "Hey, are you sure you're not getting carsick? You're as white as a ghost."

"No, I'll be fine." Molly settled back in her seat and shut her eyes, willing her stomach to settle as they turned the corner and headed towards the post office.

* * * * *

Three hours later they pulled into the driveway. The post office had been swamped and then at Burgerland, Dylan insisted on playing in the play area for a good hour after they finished eating. The sun was setting and Molly was running out of time. She flipped back the seat and began to pull bags out of the back while her mother struggled to get the unconscious toddler out of his car seat.

"Ummm, mom, can I go over to Mr. Cotton's now?"

"You know the drill. Groceries inside and put away before you take off to parts unknown. Anyway, it's getting late. Maybe you should just wait until tomorrow…"

"Pretty please? I won't be gone long. Plus, I don't have any homework, remember?"

Her mother sighed. "All right then. Just make sure to get the rest of the groceries out of the car first. I'll put them away as soon as I get Dylan inside."

As soon as Molly had carried the last bag into the house, she made a beeline to her room and dumped out the contents of her backpack onto the bed. She'd felt very strange ever since she woke up in class and it made her nervous. It took a minute before she found the word for the feeling—*unsafe*. She couldn't remember anything from that day that explained her unease. Still, it was better to take precautions and hide Clarence's feather away where nobody would ever find it. She opened the binder up and suddenly her blood ran cold. The feather was gone.

Frantically combing through her bag and double-checking the outside pockets, she fought a growing sense of dread. There was no doubt about it—the feather was nowhere to be seen. There could only be two reasons for this. She went to her jewelry box and pulled out the small vial, which held the hair from Marcus's tail. The hair still shimmered inside, indicating that her magic vision hadn't worn off. This narrowed the possibilities down to a very unsettling fact—she had somehow lost the feather at school. Replaying the day over and over in her mind, she tried to remember whether she saw it after her back pack took a spill. She recalled feeling it brush her fingers when she dug around for a pencil midway through math class. That was right before lunch, and she never needed anything else out of her pack all afternoon. She gasped, and a cold shiver ran down her back. Someone took Clarence's feather from her bag while she slept.

Fragments of a conversation bubbled to the surface of her memory, then danced away just out of reach. "Birds… she said she liked birds…" Molly murmured to herself. "…And

Griffins…" A horrible realization hit her like a punch in the stomach. *The substitute knew about the Griffin's feather.* "Oh no," she moaned. "Clarence!" She jumped to her feet and ran out of the room. She had to warn Mr. Cotton before it was too late.

CHAPTER 9

As she rounded the fence, Molly stopped in her tracks and gasped. The beautiful garden was ruined—the exotic plants ripped up by their roots and taken away. The lawn was trampled into mud. Fear planted her feet and it took her several minutes to work up the courage to walk up the broken path.

The house itself looked as if it had fared little better. The empty pet carriers that were once carefully stacked on the porch were gone, except for one or two which were broken and scattered across the lawn and driveway. The front door hung lopsidedly from one hinge, swaying gently in the breeze.

Molly saw through the open doorway that the inside of the house was a wreck as well. A mixture of horror and fear washed over her like a bucketful of icy water. A single word escaped her lips. "No…"

Just then two detectives came out on the porch, exchanging notes and shaking their heads. Molly ducked behind Mr. Cotton's battered truck, noticing that all four tires seemed to have been slashed by something with razor sharp claws.

"Guy's lost his mind," the taller of the two commented. "But do you blame him?"

"Yeah, real shame. Kids nowadays… no respect for anyone," the other agreed.

"Think this is just vandalism by some punks?"

"What else would it be? You heard him — nothing valuable was taken. Just the house and yard torn up and all his critters gone."

The tall detective scratched his head. "Hmmmmmm… Strange if you ask me. You'd think if someone was gonna trash some old coot's house and beat him up in broad daylight, at least they'd steal something."

The shorter man stepped off the porch. "Yeah, and you'd think he's get a good look at who did it. Anyway, we've been here long enough. We gotta get back if I'm gonna get the report filed before my shift's over."

Molly hung back and watched the detectives get into their car and drive off. Then she tentatively approached the house and stepped past the ruined front door.

The house was in shambles. It looked as if every piece of furniture had been picked up and thrown. Books lay shredded among broken furniture, shattered porcelain and torn curtains. The carpet was scorched in places and she noticed three broken windows and several large holes in the walls. The light fixture in the dining room had been wrenched from the ceiling and hung dangling by a single electric cord. Bits of plaster and torn wallpaper littered the ground. Mr. Cotton sat on the remnants of his couch, one leg propped up and wrapped in bandages. Large tears rolled down his cheeks. Molly couldn't remember ever seeing a grown man cry. It was scary.

"Mr. Cotton? Are you okay?"

He looked up and wiped away a tear with his sleeve. "Oh it's you, Molly,"

As she approached she noticed that her friend hadn't fared much better than his house. One eye was blackened and a long cut traveled down the side of his face. His arms were crisscrossed with scratches and bruises. She pointed to his leg. "What happened?"

He took a rumpled and somewhat wet handkerchief out of his front pocket and blew his nose. "I'm sorry you have to see me like this. It's just... just... Unthinkable!"

"What happened?" Molly repeated, trying not to sound frightened. Something was definitely not right.

"She found us. We were so careful..." He began to sob, "... So careful. We were here for so long that we assumed we were safe. We thought we had finally found a sanctuary where we could do our work undisturbed. So we let our guard down."

"We... you and Clarence, you mean?" she repeated, trying to make sense of what he was saying. She looked around, suddenly realizing the Griffin was missing. "Where's Clarence?"

Instead of answering her, he pulled out the handkerchief again and dabbed at his eyes.

Molly's voice rose in pitch. "Mr. Cotton? Where's Clarence?"

"She came and took all the creatures and then destroyed everything. My house, the gardens, the barns where we helped those who needed healing. She even polluted the pond so badly that it will be a long time before it can support life again." His grief turned to anger now. "She came sometime today in the early afternoon while I was out making my rounds," he said through clenched teeth. "He never had a chance. None of them did. When I got back her minions were taking the last of the lilies out in wheelbarrows." He laid back against the broken arm of the couch and sighed. "The lilies... Without the lilies..."

She clapped a hand to her mouth as a terrible realization hit her. "Oh no... does this mean...?"

He looked down at his feet. "Yes, Molly. Without the lilies, I won't be able to see magic any more. I'm not like you. The Sight wears off every night. By tomorrow... well..." he buried his head in his hands.

Molly suddenly felt sick to her stomach. *The strange teacher... what if...*

"Mr. Cotton?" her voice trembled. "Who is '*she*'?"

His face flushed with anger. "Eryale. She's a monster who enslaves magical creatures for her own devices. Some she sells — others come to a worse fate." He paused and looked around, as if to make sure nobody was listening. "Many of the animals staying here were rescued from her. That's why she made sure the compound was thoroughly destroyed."

Molly picked up a piece of a broken teacup. She recognized it as Clarence's favorite. The saucer lay a few feet away, smashed beyond repair next to the upturned television set. There would be no more watching game shows on it—the screen had a large hole in the center that looked like it had been made by a huge fist. She tried to banish the growing sense that was eating at her that this had something to do with the missing feather.

Mr. Cotton continued. "She disguises herself as human. Her physical appearance changes depending on her mood, but she usually looks like a tall woman with eyes that keep changing color."

"I'd be able to see what she really looks like, right?" Molly asked hopefully. "I mean, because I can see past the glamour?"

He shook his head. "I'm sorry, Molly, but her magic trumps the vision lilies. They are, after all, just flowers. The magic she uses to disguise herself is far more ancient. Even I haven't actually ever seen her true form. Clarence could see her, though," Mr. Cotton smiled sadly. "He said she resembled something the basilisk might cough up after eating a rotten piece of fish." He suddenly leaned over until his face was inches from hers. "Why do you want to know this?"

She squirmed. "I just thought if I run into the monster…"

His eyebrows furrowed. "No… That's not it. You're hiding something…" He looked deep into her eyes. "Dear God," he gasped. "You've met her already."

"NO!" she cried. "Are you sure? I came straight here from school. I couldn't have…"

"I'm positive," he insisted. "You've been *mesmerized*. I can still see some traces of her magic." He leaned back and sighed. "This isn't good. Do you remember any unusual blackouts or periods where you can't remember anything?"

"Well…" She shifted her weight from one foot to the other nervously. "I slept through lunch today. I've never done that before." She avoided his piercing gaze by looking at her shoes. "The last thing I remember was talking to the new substitute."

"A teacher… I wonder…" He paused for a moment. "No, I don't think that could have been her," he decided. "Your school was still in session when all of this happened. As powerful as she is, Eryale can't be in two places at the same time. Did you see anyone else out of the ordinary before you got to school?"

Molly shook her head and her voice dropped to a whisper. "N… no, Mr. Cotton. We had *two* substitutes today. The first one… Miss Gordon… left at lunch. The Principal told us she had a family emergency. We had a different sub all afternoon."

He frowned. "I see. What I don't understand is how she would have chosen to mesmerize you in the first place."

She stared at the spot where the piece of plaster landed, too embarrassed to meet his gaze. Her stomach knotted up, but she had to tell him the truth. "I think I know," she replied sadly. She told him about the feather and how it was missing. "Miss Gordon must have seen it when my binder fell out of my backpack," she explained, trying hard to hold back the tears that were beginning to well up in her eyes. "I don't remember telling her anything about Clarence or you. But the feather was gone when I got home… and then… *this*." She burst out sobbing.

The old man closed his eyes and took a long deep breath. "There, there. You're only a kid. You never had a chance. You didn't even know she existed before now." His rage began to boil again and his voice rose in pitch and volume. "Of course she'd find out everything she wanted to know from you. There's no way you could defend yourself." He started to rise from the couch but winced in pain. "However, you're not completely without blame," he growled. "You should never have taken one of Clarence's feathers. You provided Euryale with a very strong weapon against us. She used the feather to get past our protective spells. Once she was inside…" he motioned around him and shook his head with a sigh.

"I'm sorry, Mr. Cotton," she moaned. "I'll make it better… somehow."

"I'm afraid there is nothing you can do," he replied. "She's enslaved all of the creatures and who knows what she'll do to them. As for Clarence, he and Euryale are old foes, so I don't think she'll be very kind to him."

"I'll get him back. And rescue the others… somehow."

"No, Molly, I can't allow that. It's too dangerous. This isn't some little bedtime story with monsters that flee when you turn on the light. This is real." He unwrapped the bandage on his leg. "She left me with this parting gift," he groaned through clenched teeth.

She gasped. His leg was swollen to twice its normal size and an angry shade of red. In the middle of his shin there was a large welt that looked like a sting from some kind of enormous bee. "Oh my goodness," she exclaimed. "She did that?"

He nodded and started to wind the bandages back around his leg. "I'm afraid this is nothing. She's capable of so much more. There's really no way you can do anything."

"What about the constable? Can't we call her?"

He looked miserable. "I'm afraid not. The Magical Compliance Department only deals with interactions between magic and non-magic entities. Since Euryale is magic and only took away only plants and animals with magic properties, I'm afraid the constable can't do anything in this situation."

"That's ridiculous."

"It's typical government bureaucracy."

"So what do we do?"

"You can't do anything. I need to make contact with some of my friends and see if I can get them to help." He lay back on the couch. "Of course this is going to slow me down a bit."

Molly bit her lip as she looked around at the mess. "Can I at least come over and help you until your leg is better? I'm sure mom won't mind."

He looked relieved. "Yes, I'd like that. But let's start fresh tomorrow after you come home from school."

She looked at the door hanging haphazardly from a single bent hinge. "Umm, do you think we should do anything about that?"

"No. Just leave it be. I'll find someone to fix it in the morning." He sounded tired and withdrawn.

"Okay, well… I guess goodnight then. See you tomorrow." She carefully adjusted the door back into place and stepped off the porch. Everything seemed so quiet now and this made her uncomfortable. She realized how accustomed she had become to the chatter of the magical flora and fauna at Mr. Cotton's house. Now there was nothing but the rustle of the wind through the fronds of the palm trees that lined her street. She stopped, thinking she had just seen a strange black hairy creature wearing dirty white sneakers peeking out from behind a tree across the street. But when she looked again, there was nothing but swaying shadows of the palm trees.

CHAPTER 10

The next afternoon, Molly dashed home from school and over to her neighbor's house. She found Mr. Cotton sitting in a rocking chair with his bandaged leg resting on a dented animal carrier. Occasionally he barked an order to the two young men stacking broken furniture in a large pile at the far end of the driveway. They looked up, shook their heads in confusion and went back to working.

"Mr. Cotton!" she exclaimed as she ran up to him.

"Darn kids," he griped. "I should have told them to leave the music players at home. Those earphones make them deaf as a pair of stone dragons!"

"It's Miss Gordon… She was back in school today! What am I going to do?"

The old man raised his finger to his lips. He pointed to the door, indicating that the conversation could only continue in the safety of the house. It took a lot of effort on his part and a little help from Molly to extract himself from the chair and hobble inside.

"Molly," he reprimanded her once the door was shut. "What did I tell you about being careful? She has spies everywhere. It's not safe for us to discuss anything concerning her or Clarence while out in the open." He limped into the kitchen and collapsed into a slightly battered chair in the eating alcove. "Please, can you get me a soda?"

She opened the refrigerator, took out a can of Mountain Dew and handed it to him. "But what about Miss Gordon? I just know she was planning to keep me in during lunch again... alone."

"We can't be sure of that," he warned. "But I can tell you this. She's going to be watching you carefully. You need to make sure not to let on that you know who she is. It's dangerous enough that she knows you have the Sight!" He shifted his weight in the chair and grimaced.

She noticed dark puffy circles under his eyes and he looked a lot more tired than he did when she arrived. "Are you okay?"

He sighed. "I'm afraid this was no ordinary injury. It's really taken a toll on me. But that's not the worst part... I can't see magic anymore."

"Are you sure?"

"Of course I'm sure," he snapped. "The first thing I did this morning was test myself. I hoped that maybe by some miracle I'd be wrong and the Sight would somehow be there... but alas..."

Molly stared at a piece of plaster on the floor, not really knowing what to say. Then a thought occurred to her. "Your friends—the ones you said could help. Can't they help you get your Sight back?"

"No, unfortunately they can't... or won't. They don't concern themselves with everyday problems of humans. They're very clear about that. I won't even ask them to help me with getting my Sight back."

"Well that's stupid. Why even bother finding them?"

He sighed. "They're the only hope we have now. They won't give me back the Sight, but they will help us against Euryale. Each one of them has their own grudge with that monster. Plus, each owes me a favor. They can't turn a blind eye to us."

"Okay. So how do we reach them? I mean, they don't have phones or emails, do they?"

He smiled sadly. "No, magic creatures tend to shun technology for the most part. They prefer to do business in person. I need to find someway to reach them..."

"I could go for you," she chirped.

"No, child. That's impossible. I can't send a *little* girl…"

"I'm not little and I have my skateboard and a bus pass. That's gotta count for something."

He looked at her for a long time without saying anything. Finally he spoke in a low whisper. "I guess there's no other option. But first…" He reached into his pocket and removed something, which he held in a closed fist. Slowly he opened his hand. "What's in my hand?"

"A tiny shoe," she replied. "It's gold and curls up where the toes are. Like a genie slipper or something."

He nodded. "Good. That means the lily juice is still working on you. Otherwise there'd be no point in this conversation going any further. Let's keep our fingers crossed that it stays with you until you're able to find my friends." He turned the slipper over in his fingers before returning it to his pocket. "The shoe actually belongs to one of the members of an interesting family of sprites that lives in the wall behind the English Literature section in the public library. About once a year or so they throw a huge party and I usually get called in by an irate librarian to 'exterminate' the 'mice.' 'Course I don't know what will happen next time…"

"We'll find Clarence—and the lilies will come back. And you'll be able to see magic again! I just know you will."

He sighed. "I hope you're right."

Molly scratched her ear and her tone became more solemn. "I used to hear all kinds of whispering when I was here. Now everything's quiet. Do you think the magic's starting to wear off?"

He looked beyond her to a point outside of the window. "You don't hear anything because there aren't any voices to hear. What you heard before were the conversations of the flowers. They're all gone now…"

He stood for a moment, lost in thought. Molly was keenly aware of the silence and the destruction that she was ultimately responsible for. She wanted to cry.

"Now, we have a lot of work to do," he announce, completely changing the subject and breaking the tension. "You'll need to find three of my friends."

"Are they lost here in this world too?"

"No, these are very powerful creatures who have their own reasons for staying in our world. They are most definitely not lost."

"But they'll know I'm coming, right? You'll tell them."

He shook his head. "I can't speak for what they do and do not know, but I'm sure they know of you already. But I won't be able to alert them of your visit. Even if there was some way for me to reach them, it wouldn't do any good."

"Huh?"

"It's a magic thing," he tried to explain. "Magic folk are very set in their ways, especially where humans are concerned. They will test you, but once you've proved yourself to them, they should be fairly helpful."

"So, how do I prove myself?"

"They will each ask you a series of questions or to perform some type of task. It's very medieval, but that's how they like to do it. If you pass they will each give you something that will help you defeat Euryale."

"Oh, okay. Like a riddle." Her eyes narrowed suspiciously. "And what if I don't prove myself? Will they eat me?"

Mr. Cotton laughed. "Oh, dear, of course not! This isn't a storybook where the fairy godfather sends the heroine to go face down a fire-breathing dragon. The worst thing that could possibly happen would be that you fail and they refuse to help. You won't be in any real life-threatening danger." His voice grew somber again. "Of course if you fail, we will be in a pickle. If you can't pass their tests, they won't give us the help we need."

"It' ll be all right," Molly said quickly, mostly to reassure herself. "I'll be fine. I can do this."

"You are a brave girl." He ruffled the top of her head. "I wish I could go—at least part of the way—but you have to seek them out and face them alone. Being able to successfully find each of them and get them to talk to you is a test in itself."

She straightened herself to her full height. "I'm ready, Mr. Cotton," she said with determination. "Where do I start?"

"Tomorrow, after school, you'll go find the first of our allies... the Sphinx." He reached inside his shirt and drew out a deep green stone flecked with little spots of bright red, set into a simple silver bezel and suspended from a leather cord. "This is a heliotrope," he explained as he untied the cord and held it out to her. "It's also known as a bloodstone. Legend has it that the flecks of red come from dragon's blood..." He trailed off as he saw the puzzled expression on her face. "I suppose the history of the name doesn't really matter. The Sphinx will recognize it. He gave it to me a long time ago as a symbol of a promise he made to me."

She fastened the cord around her neck and tucked the pendant into her shirt.

"Good." he said, nodding with approval. "When the time comes, it's absolutely imperative that you remember to show that stone to the Sphinx—otherwise he might not help us, even if you do pass his test. He's quite proud and doesn't grant favors lightly."

"So where do I find him?"

"He lives in Union Station... in downtown Los Angeles. You'll have to take the commuter train from the platform on State Street. It goes straight to Union Station. Have you ever been on the train?"

"No," she answered him, trying to conceal her fear. "But I've taken buses around town hundreds of times. How much different can it be?"

"Taking the train is easier than the bus. All you have to do is ride it to the end of the line. That's Union Station. When you get off the train, find the old ticket hall where the Southwest Chief still boards. That's where you'll find the Sphinx..." His eyes twinkled. "Or he might just find you. I don't know what form he takes these days. It's been many years since I last saw him. But if I know anything about the Sphinx it's that he's no introvert. Just keep your eyes peeled and look out for anything out of the ordinary. When he's ready, he'll reveal himself to you, one way or another."

Molly thanked him and turned to go. As she was exiting through the front door he called out to her. "Hold on a second, you'll need this." He waved a rumpled slip of yellow paper at her. She returned and he pressed it into her hand.

She looked at the battered ticket. It was dated September 25, 1975 9:57 AM. The unmistakable words '*Good for One Way on the Date Shown*' was printed right under the destination.

"Umm, I'm not sure this ticket will work, Mr. Cotton." She tried to hand it back, but he waved her away.

"Nonsense, Molly. Of course it will work," he insisted.

She eyed the ticket again and noticed something else. "Is this for the right Union Station? This says Chicago…"

He began to chuckle. "The ticket's enchanted. You're just seeing through the glamour cast on it. Don't worry, if a conductor asks for it, he'll see a valid ticket with today's date and the correct destination." He winked at her. "Just make sure you don't lose it. The last thing we need is a transit official to run across a magic train ticket."

She tucked it safely in her front pocket.

"Now remember. You won't have much time. It's an hour ride each way and you *absolutely* must make the 4:40 train leaving Union Station if you are planning on getting back before your mother misses you. I'd really prefer you catch one even sooner. Downtown Los Angeles is not a very safe place for little girls after dark."

Molly nodded her head in agreement "Okay Mr. Cotton. I promise. And I will come straight here when I get back so you won't have to worry." With that she left through the front door, pausing once on the path to wave at him.

* * * *

Barnaby watched her go from the front window, brows furrowed. He couldn't let the girl know how much he was worried for her. The Sphinx could be extremely unpredictable and he would never have sent her alone under any other circumstances. He just hoped Molly could pass whatever test the Sphinx had in store. He rolled up his pants leg and examined the discolored area that now extended past the bandage. Dark spidery tendrils snaked up his leg to the knee and down into his sock. The poison was spreading.

CHAPTER 11

The train ride was just as Mr. Cotton promised—completely uneventful and much easier than riding a bus. For one thing, Molly noted, the seats were a lot more comfortable and there were a lot more of them, so nobody had to stand. The train was also smoother and devoid of the constant rattle and shaking of buses. Finally the people riding the train looked… well… *friendlier* than bus riders. They were relaxed and spent the trip working on laptops or reading. She found a seat across from an elderly woman who called her 'a brave girl' and offered to share her newspaper. Thanking her, Molly grabbed the comics and curled up in the seat next to the window.

Exactly fifty-seven minutes later the train rolled into Downtown Los Angeles. Molly exited the train and was swept along with a sea of passengers into the station. She looked around in a panic until she saw a sign for the Southwest Chief pointing away from the direction the crowd favored. The rest of the throng continued towards the newer part of the station where she supposed buses and subways would whisk them to other parts of the city.

As she traveled farther down the hallway, the clamor from the noisy travelers receded until all that was left was the soft flip flop of her sneakers on the concrete floor. She glanced down, noticing that the cement was colored to look like a geometric pattern. Just as she registered this, she rounded a corner and the concrete sharply ended in a field of colorful stone tiles in the same pattern.

She stopped and looked up to see a majestic archway carved to look like something out of a Greek temple. Beyond it was a vast room with rows of large comfortable, leather-upholstered chairs. She was now in the oldest part of the station. *This must be the ticket hall,* she thought.

She wandered aimlessly, looking around for something unusual. The station was quiet in the afternoon—a few people milled around waiting for the next train or otherwise killing time. She looked for some kind of sign that one of them might be the elusive Sphinx, but wasn't sure how to tell without actually asking. She saw a pair of teenagers with their hair dyed matching shades of neon green, blue and red. Mr. Cotton hadn't mentioned anything about the Sphinx being with anyone, so she ruled them out. She saw a tiny man, shorter than she was, leading a towering great Dane loaded down with saddlebags like a small packhorse. Both looked promising, but when she approached them, the dog growled and the small man glared at her and quickened his pace. She saw a bald man with piercing eyes lined with heavy black eyeliner, dressed in a shiny black vinyl coat, black tights and patent-leather combat boots. He looked like the kind of person her mother always warned her not to talk to, so she left him alone. She saw a lot of strange people, but no one looked like a Sphinx.

Then she saw the cat.

She couldn't remember seeing a more magnificent creature. He was the kind of oversized orange tabby more likely to be found lazing about in a suburban home rather than wandering around a train station. With his sleek fur and stocky build he certainly wasn't a hungry stray, nor did he have that skittish way about him that cats have when they are in unfamiliar settings. In fact, he looked quite at home in the station. As she watched him prowl around the room, looking for something interesting to hunt, she noticed that nobody seemed to think it particularly strange that a cat should have taken up residence in Union Station. In fact, he was completely ignored, even by the great

Dane, who passed within a few feet without even acknowledging the feline.

Nobody seems to notice… as if they can't even see him, she thought to herself. Then she realized with a shock that she had found what she was looking for.

The tomcat caught hold of a cockroach, sniffed it and then let it go. It scurried a few feet, only to be trapped once more. The feline lifted his paw slowly and examined the bug with an expression of distaste. Molly waited for him to release the insect again like cats often did. Instead he extended one long claw and cruelly impaled the bug through the thorax. Molly gasped. The tabby lifted his paw and watched with interest as the cockroach squirmed at the end of his claw. Finally, when the last leg stopped twitching, the cat flicked the dead insect off and sent it skittering across the polished marble floor. Then he leapt up onto the back of the nearest empty chair and began to lick a paw until he spotted Molly watching him. Their eyes met and both were still for a moment while they sized one another up.

Molly wasn't sure what to make of the animal. Obviously he was magic, since it seemed he was invisible to everyone in the station. She figured her Sight was the only reason she could see him, especially since he was now glaring at her as if she had somehow intruded on his privacy just by seeing him. Mr. Cotton hadn't said much about the Sphinx, but she assumed he would be friendly. This creature was definitely not benevolent, if his behavior towards the cockroach was any indicator.

Maybe it's one of Ms. Gordon's spies, she thought in a sudden panic. It hadn't occurred to her until that moment that she might run into another creature besides the Sphinx in Union Station. *How stupid of me! Of course she would know Mr. Cotton would seek out help. She probably has spies all over the place.*

The cat hopped off the chair and approached her. He strode purposefully in the kind of feline manner that would have been quite threatening had he been the size or a lion or tiger. However, as he was only a house cat, he mostly looked determined. Still,

Molly took a step back. She wasn't sure what powers a magic cat might possess.

"It not be nice to stare'," he remarked in a deep, heavily-accented baritone. He jumped up on the nearest chair as cats often do to be high enough to conduct a polite conversation.

"You can talk!" she exclaimed.

"Well, of course I can," he replied somewhat peevishly, his Caribbean twang becoming more pronounced. "What you be expectin'?"

"Sorry," she apologized, completely taken aback. "But you're… a… a cat!"

He laid his ears back and narrowed his eyes. "Who be you?" he asked suspiciously, choosing, in catlike fashion, not to acknowledge her last remark.

"My name is Molly…" She trailed off. *Stupid, stupid, stupid,* she silently chided herself. *Now he knows my name and that I can see him.* It was too late to do anything about it so she continued. "I'm sorry if I was rude before but I didn't think I'd see a cat here, especially one who talks."

The tomcat looked around and noticed one or two people beginning to take interest. "Shhhh," he hissed. "Keep your voice down, girl. You be attractin' attention." He nodded his head towards a businessman glancing up from his newspaper at Molly, a mixture of curiosity and concern on his face. "If you be lucky," the cat continued, "they assume you a mutterer and leave you alone. If luck not be with you and some bad person come…" he trailed off without finishing his sentence.

She quickly turned her attention to her tennis shoes until she saw the man lower his head into his paper.

"Sit," he motioned with a paw towards the seat of the chair he was perched on. "Dis way it not look like you talkin' to da empty chair."

She blushed and sat down quickly. "Thanks," she whispered. "What's a mutterer?"

He rolled his eyes in exasperation but otherwise ignored the question. "Look straight... not at me. Act like you be waitin' for your parents or sometin." He scanned the quiet station and then relaxed when he was sure there was nobody watching them. "Humans don't normally be seein' me," he continued in a patronizing manner.

"R... right," she stammered.

"Hmmmmm, so's you got da Sight, which means somebody be givin' it to ya. What you be here for? Little ones like you don't be comin' here by demselves 'less they be runnin' from sometin or lost..." He peered at her with his big golden eyes. Molly felt like she understood what the cockroach might have been feeling right before it was stabbed. "...And unless me eye be wrong, you ain't neither," he concluded, with a slightly menacing tone to his voice.

"I'm not," she answered quietly. "I was sent here... to find someone."

"Sent?" the cat looked incredulous. "Why? And who be sendin' a little girl into dis dangerous place all alone?"

"Mr. Cotton told me to come here. It's important," she answered and immediately wanted to kick herself for answering the cat.

"And why would dis Mr.Cotton do dis? It not be safe here. Surely he know dis."

She looked up at the large clock. It was almost 4 P.M. Time was getting short and at this point she was no closer to her goal than when she arrived in the station. *If nothing else, this cat has to know everything that goes on here.* She decided to throw caution to the wind. "I have to find the Sphinx," she admitted. "Mr. Cotton said he owed him a favor and would help me. He'd come himself but he got hurt and can't walk. Do you know where I might find him?"

"Hmmmph," the cat snorted. "And why should da Sphinx believe you?"

Shame burned her face. It hadn't occurred to her that anyone would question her, least of all the creature she was searching for. "I guess he might not believe me," she answered and pulled the heliotrope from inside her shirt. "Maybe that's why Mr. Cotton gave me this to show him."

His eyes narrowed. "I knows dis stone and da man dat owns it," he murmured, "I know da favor you be speakin' of and who it owed to…" He descended onto her lap to get a better look at the necklace dangling from her fingers. "…But dat be a long time ago and he go by Jonas Merriweather back den. Hmmmm… Cotton… me don't know dat name, but it don't matter none. Da favor owed anyhow."

"So you know the Sphinx? Will you take me to him?"

"Silly girl," he chuckled as he jumped off her lap. "I can't be takin' you to da Sphinx anymore than you be takin' me to your left ear. For I be he, and he be me."

She was never sure afterwards whether the change in his size was due to the fact that he stripped off the glamour hiding him from her, or if he was always that big and she just didn't notice it before. Whatever the case he seemed to simultaneously grow and transform from a cat into a very strange creature. She had read about Sphinxes and so expected to see something out of the ordinary. However, she was not quite prepared for his peculiar appearance, which was nothing like the pictures or statues she'd seen all her life. Instead of beautiful chiseled features like those depicted by Greek and Roman artists, the Sphinx wore a round coffee-colored face that reflected character rather than beauty. He had amber-colored eyes, a wide flat nose and a large mouth with soft dark lips split where a cat's normally were. Instead of a majestic Egyptian or Babylonian headdress, he wore a red, yellow and green knitted beanie to confine a tangle of bright orange dreadlocks. Although he did have the body of a lion, his furry rotund gut almost touched to the ground. Several strings of wooden beads and a large pendant bearing the emblem of a lion hung around his neck.

"Surprised?" He grinned. "Perhaps you be 'spectin' sometin like dat?" he asked, pointing to a pair of marble statues on the opposite side of the room, flanking the entrance to the platform. She nodded dumbly. He sat back on his haunches and roared with laughter. "Humans be such funny creatures! 'Magine da Sphinx lookin' like dose statues!"

The clock chimed four times, reminding her that it was getting late. She mustered up all the courage she had and looked him straight in the eyes. "Mr. Cotton said you would test me to see if I'm worthy," she said nervously, changing the subject. "I know a little about you—I guess you're going to give me a riddle to solve and if I don't answer the question correctly you'll eat me, right?"

His smile vanished and he fixed his deep golden eyes on her, as if examining her soul for flaws. He looked menacing in the same way a cat looks the moment before it pounces on a mouse. Molly was tempted to run back to the train, go home and admit defeat. Instead she took a chance and stood her ground. If she was going to be too frightened to face the Sphinx's test, she would never be able to defeat Miss Gordon and save Clarence.

After an uncomfortable pause, he broke the silence. "Girl, me thinks you be readin' too many stories." His eyes crinkled with mirth. "Who tol' you da Sphinx be askin' you a riddle? Der be better ways of testin' a person's true nature, than askin' a riddle."

"Well… yeah… I guess so," she stammered, completely taken aback at his candor. "It always did seem dumb to me that the hero could pass a test of courage just by knowing the answer to some dumb riddle. It just meant that someone gave him the answer before, not that he was really brave or anything."

The Sphinx laughed again. "That be me thinkin' too. But humans—they write about what dey want to and pay no mind to common sense. That why dey be callin' it *fiction…*'" He trailed off for a minute and frowned. "As for eatin' you…" he growled menacingly and paused for dramatic effect. "Little girls be too gamey for me likin'… least most of da time." He flashed a big smile full of sharp knife-like teeth.

For once in her life she didn't mind that someone didn't find her appetizing. She relaxed a little, but still scooted back farther into the chair. "If you're not going to make me answer a riddle, how will I prove my worth?" she asked.

"Already done, mon," he replied. "It take a strong will to come here to find me not knowin' what you be findin', but knowin' it be dangerous if you fail. You looked me straight in da eyes and answered me truthful like, even when you thought me might be eatin' you. You a brave, smart girl. Jonas be wise sendin' you."

Molly was speechless. She didn't know what to say to that. She had been expecting a more challenging trial. This was too easy. She almost asked the Sphinx if that was it, but then thought better of it. *Best not to try my luck*, she thought.

"Hmmmmmm… maybe you be willin' to help me with sometin' before you go?" the Sphinx casually asked. "Outside der be a garden with thirteen rose bushes. Perhaps you be a good girl and bring me back one flower from each bush?"

She nodded. She started to walk towards a pair of brass-accented glass doors that led to the courtyard outside.

"Oh, one more tin,'" the Sphinx called after her. "Da bushes, dey not be tended to for a bit now. Don't be givin' dem too much. A drop or two be enough. No more."

Molly turned to ask him what he meant but the Sphinx had disappeared. She turned back and pushed against the massive doors until they opened. She felt rather than saw a funny shimmering sensation as she passed through the doorway—almost as if she were walking into a mirage. However, it disappeared as soon as she stepped outside into a small deserted courtyard.

CHAPTER 12

Despite the bustle of the station, the courtyard looked as if nobody had visited it in years. Molly glanced back to see if the Sphinx was watching her, but the doors had closed behind her and the glare of the afternoon sun reflecting on the glass obscured everything inside. She followed a litter-strewn gravel path into a winding maze of boxwood hedges. The hedges got taller and taller until they towered over her and blocked out all of the noise of the city. Soon everything was silent except the soft crunch of her sneakers on the small pebbles.

After a few minutes, she turned a corner and the path opened up into a circular garden. A small birdbath stood cock-eyed in the center, choked with dead leaves and stained with years of neglect. A small stone sphinx perched on the edge of the basin as if gazing at its own reflection (if there had been water). A circle of blackened, thorny canes surrounded the birdbath, the only remnants left of the rosebushes she was looking for. She sighed. There was no sign of life, let alone the thirteen roses the Sphinx asked for. She imagined what the garden must have looked like and wondered when he had last seen it.

Walking around the garden, she searched for some indication of life, but there was nothing. Weeds grew among the dead roses, very almost completely choking them out in places. Stepping over a tuft of foxtails to get a better look at the stone birdbath, she tripped when one of the thorny canes caught on the cuff of her pants. She put out her hand to catch herself and landed on a thorny branch.

"OWW!" she exclaimed as she got up. A small thorn had embedded itself into her right thumb. Pulling it out opened a cut which started to bleed. A single drop of blood fell onto one of the dead canes of the nearest rosebush. Molly stuck her finger in her mouth like a hurt toddler while she brushed the debris from her clothes.

A rustling noise suddenly caught her attention and she looked down. The stem splashed with her blood was moving as if shaken by an unseen force. Color pumped like blood through the cane and traveled down its length and spread. Fat buds popped out of nodules on the branches and quickly unfurled to become new leaves. Within minutes a lush green rosebush stood in place of the lifeless branches. The shrub swayed as if buffered by a strong wind as it filled out. Flower buds appeared and swelled on stems that lengthened and thickened. Soon Molly was looking at a bush full of the most beautiful long-stemmed yellow roses she had ever seen. It looked completely out of place in the otherwise wasted garden. Although not exactly sure how this happened, she was pretty sure that magic was involved. She looked at the roses and then at her finger, which was still slowly oozing blood.

"*A drop or two…*"

She now understood what the Sphinx meant. Blood made the roses come to life. She counted exactly thirteen flowers. "I wonder if it would be okay if I just picked these," she commented out loud. "No," she answered herself, "I promised I'd pick one rose from each plant." Squeezing her thumb, she held it over the next dead bush in the circle. Managing to coax another drop of blood from the cut on her finger, she let it drop onto a dry leaf. It shuddered and turned green as the blood brought it back to life. This bush repeated the same incredible transformation as its predecessor, this time producing a profusion of white roses that glowed like they were lit from within.

Molly now realized this was the Sphinx's test. The rosebushes were each a different color. "Crafty old cat. I'll bet he knew there'd be thirteen roses on each bush," she observed. By insisting on one bloom from each plant, the Sphinx made the stakes a little higher. She had to revive all of them.

She broke off a thorn and used it to open up the cut on her finger a little wider. Moving from plant to plant she smeared blood on a dead leaf, a black cane, a withered dead flower. Each time the result was the same. The plants all came to life until she was looking at thirteen bushes with beautiful roses of every color imaginable. Some were like roses she was used to—respectable shades of red, pink, white, orange or yellow. But then there were also otherworldly shades of electric blue, violet and even lime green.

Stepping to the first bush—the one with rich golden flowers—she plucked one perfect bloom and held it close, inhaling the strong fruity perfume that reminded her of summer days on her beloved Maui. She stepped to the next bush and broke off a single white rose as delicate as meringue with a scent reminiscent of honeysuckle. She paused and savored the scent of the two flowers together.

Suddenly she heard a rustle from the first bush and glanced over, horrified. It was wilting before her eyes. It seemed as if it was reaching its branches out to her like a man dying of thirst. She rushed over and squeezed another drop from her aching finger. The rose revived quickly and even grew higher before her eyes. Its flowers were even more spectacular, dwarfing the bloom she held in her hand.

She contemplated picking a new one, and as if reading her mind, the yellow rose in her hand drooped as soon as the second batch of flowers opened. She dropped the dying flower and picked a new one. There was a sigh and another rustle behind her. She wheeled around to see the rosebush with white roses begin to wither almost on cue, so she stepped over to it and fed it another drop of blood. Like its sister, the white rosebush also grew taller and set even more beautiful roses. Molly picked another replacement for the one in her hand that now was already beginning to wilt.

One by one, the rosebushes died in turn, some almost as soon as she finished picking a flower. Molly revived them with blood from her pricked finger and each time the bushes grew taller and the flowers bigger, while the previous blooms picked from the plant wilted and died in her hands. Round and round she went in a wild circle of tending to the roses. They seemed to wilt more quickly now but recover even faster. She rushed from bush to bush, tending to the roses and picking new flowers to replace those in her bouquet that were dying. The fully opened flowers were now as big as serving dishes and a single petal was larger than Molly's hand. Her bouquet was getting heavy and hard to manage. She was tiring quickly so she paused for a moment to catch her breath.

The strong perfume from the roses made her feel lightheaded and she thought a nap seemed like a nice treat right now. Fallen rose petals were forming drifts where the warm afternoon breeze gently gathered them in corners and against the foot of the birdbath. She looked at them, thinking about lying down with her head cradled in roses softer than feathers. The huge blossoms nodded in approval and dropped more fragrant petals on her.

Mr. Cotton's warning echoed somewhere in the back of her mind. *"You absolutely must make the 4:40 train…"*

She looked up with a start and realized the sun was a lot lower in the sky than it had been when she first entered the garden. Glancing at her watch, she realized it had stopped at 4:07. That was about the time *I walked out to the courtyard*, she thought to herself. She needed to get back. She quickly counted thirteen roses in her fingers that would send the most discerning florist into fits of jealousy. But she didn't want to leave. She had an overpowering urge to stay just a little longer and feed the roses one more drop—to pick yet one better flower than what she had…

It took all of her willpower to walk away.

As soon as she left the circle, the thirteen rosebushes withered with a sigh and died in a split second. Molly looked down at the bunch of flowers in her hands, expecting to them wilt and die as well, but they still looked fresh and alive. A sudden strong wind swept through the garden and faded rose petals were lifted into the air like paper butterflies and blown away. Soon nothing was left except dead and blackened canes in a weed-choked and forgotten garden.

CHAPTER 13

Molly found the Sphinx dozing in cat form on the back of a chair. When he heard her enter, he opened one eye and stretched. She held out the bouquet of flowers with a triumphant look on her face.

He frowned at the massive blooms. "What I be tellin' you 'bout dem roses, girl?" he reprimanded her. "One or two drops, no more. You fed dem too much." He hopped down, transforming as his paws touched the floor.

"I tried to do what you told me," she explained, "but they kept wilting. Every time I gave them more, they would grow bigger and bigger roses..." she trailed off as she noticed anger clouding his face. "I thought you would like the giant flowers," she whimpered.

He shook his head. "You be needin' to open your ears, girl. Good ting you remembered da words of de old Sphinx in time. Had you not stopped feedin' dem when you did, dey'd put da sleeping spell on you and sucked you dry."

She thought back to how she almost fell asleep in the garden. "You mean I could have died?" she asked with alarm.

"No, no, no," he replied with a dangerous gleam in his cat eyes. "Dat only be happenin' if you da kind of little one who don't be followin' directions. You not dat kind of little one... Are ya, girl?" He cocked his head sideways and eyed her suspiciously.

She looked at her feet and squirmed. Then she heard him let out a soft chuckle. She glanced up. His wide grin was back and his eyes twinkled.

"Come close now, I got sometin' for you," he purred.

"Is this the talisman Mr. Cotton said would help me get Clarence back?"

"Might be," he replied with the hint of a question in his voice. "You still got da heliotrope, yes?"

She nodded.

"Take it off so's I can be seein' it."

She unfastened the black cord and held the necklace out to him. He took it in his cupped paws and blew gently. Molly gasped in wonder as the pendant ignited with a blue fire. The flame spread along the length of the cord, burning brightly for a few moments, until with a crackle and a snap, the flames extinguished, leaving a pile of ash. The Sphinx shook the black powder away, revealing something sparkling in his great palm. Molly saw that the dark green stone was now a beautiful teardrop-shaped topaz set in silver filigree, hanging on a delicate silver chain. It was the same deep rich golden color as his eyes.

"Da stone now be your talisman and with it you got da protection of da Sphinx. It be givin' you da courage to face your greatest fears," he explained as he returned it to her. She took the necklace and fastened it around her neck. It felt strangely cool against her skin, as if it had been in a freezer instead of engulfed in flames only a few moments before. The great beast gave her a playful cuff on the top of her head. "Now go on back to Jonas Merriweather and tell him me repaying' da debt owed 'im." He paused for a moment and a look of concern came over his face. "As for you; you be travelin' down a long, dark road. Watch your back and remember: *Sometimes da smallest ting be da most important.*"

With that he gave a flick of his tail and turned himself back into a cat. "Now go on. Your train be leavin' in ten minutes and you be wantin' Platform 7B." He lifted a paw and pointed towards one of the tunnels.

"How did you know?"

The cat just sauntered away with his tail making a question mark. She glanced up at the ornate clock and saw that he was right. She turned and hurried out of the room.

* * * *

The Sphinx watched her go until she was out of sight. Then he noticed something out of the corner of his eye. The shape that emerged from the shadows and set after her set his fur on edge. His tail bristled and he gave a low hiss, but by now Molly was too far down the corridor to notice. There was no way to warn her now—he could only hope that she was indeed as smart and resourceful as she seemed. *Otherwise...* he shook his head to dislodge the unpleasant vision that entered his mind.

* * * *

Molly boarded the train and found a seat near the back of the car. She shivered, a sudden image materializing in her mind of a snake wearing a chicken suit hiding under the seat behind her. Fear sent paralyzing fingers of ice through her body. She touched the talisman around her neck and mustered enough courage to turn around, only to come face to face with an empty row of seats. Whatever it was must have only been a figment of her overactive imagination. *Yes, that's it,* she consoled herself as she settled back into her seat. There was a soft swoosh as the car doors shut and a lurch as the train began to move.

CHAPTER 14

The next day, Molly entered the classroom and groaned as she spotted Miss Gordon at the front of the room. Even though the substitute had made it perfectly clear she would be teaching the class for the next several weeks, Molly still harbored some hope that Mr. Robinson would make a surprise recovery or that another teacher would take over. Fighting the urge to hide in the fact, she marched down the center aisle and took a desk two rows back from the front. The teacher peered up over her wire frame glasses with interest. Molly squared her shoulders and looked directly at Miss Gordon. "Good morning," she chirped.

"Molly, why don't you come sit up here next to me today." Miss Gordon pointed at the desk in the front of the classroom. The class muttered and whispered amongst themselves. They were getting used to this ritual between their classmate and this odd new substitute, although many wondered what made Molly so special.

Instead of bowing her head in embarrassment and slinking to the front of the room as she might have done the day before, Molly cheerfully changed seats. She extracted a pencil and a spiral bound notebook from her backpack and placed them on the desk in front of her. The she looked up expectantly at her teacher and waited.

Miss Gordon narrowed her eyes. It was clear that Molly's change in behavior bothered her immensely.

The class seemed to pick up on the new and improved Molly too. During History, Tommy Woodbury, the most popular boy in school, asked her if she knew the answer for the essay question from the homework the night before. Molly hadn't finished the assignment so, Tiffany Washington, widely regarded as the smartest girl in class, leaned over and offered to help her catch up during lunch. Miss Gordon picked on Molly several times and asked her difficult questions, but even when she got the answers wrong, nobody snickered or whispered. In fact, it seemed that the class was now on her side.

"Molly," Miss Gordon asked, "can you please tell me what major role Venice played in the *Black Death*?"

Molly drew a blank stare as she rose. Tiffany flipped through her history book and then raised her hand.

"Tiffany, I'm sure you know the answer from your reading," the substitute addressed her sternly, "but I specifically asked Molly to answer the question."

"I think what Tiffany is trying to tell you, Miss Gordon," Molly explained, "is that there's no mention of Venice in our history book. Our book only covers American history."

Several students giggled.

"Of course, what was I thinking?" The substitute replied. "How could I possibly expect you to know something not mentioned in your history book."

Molly smiled and began to sit down.

"Not yet, young lady. I'm not finished with you. Since you have so wisely pointed out my error, I would like you to write a three page report on the subject. Due…" She tapped one perfectly manicured finger on the side of her cheek, "…tomorrow…" She looked over at Tiffany, "…at the beginning of class."

Molly collapsed into her chair. 'The Black Death?' She wasn't even sure she knew what Miss Gordon was talking about. There was no way she could research the material and write a report in a day. There was no Internet connection at the house and even if there was, Dylan had spilled grape juice into the keyboard of their computer three weeks ago, effectively killing it. Her mother promised about once a week to get it fixed, but so far had not taken it in to the repair shop. The computers at the public library were always full, with usually at least a three-day waiting list. Researching the topic in a day without any warning was going to be next to impossible.

As if she could read Molly's thoughts, Miss Gordon smiled triumphantly at her. "I have a great suggestion. Perhaps you should use the computer here during lunch and after school to do your research. Of course I would have to be here with you, but I don't mind staying after school if it helps further the education of one of my students."

Molly nodded her head. *So that's it*, she thought to herself. *She wants to get me alone again to mesmerize me.* She smiled and nodded, while simultaneously dreaming up possible ways to get out of this dilemma.

"Then it's settled," Miss Gordon concluded. "You will stay after school with me for as long as it takes for you to get the necessary information for your report."

The bell rang, announcing lunch and the class piled out of the room. But instead of being left alone, Molly found herself surrounded by new friends. Her plight seemed to have an effect on her classmates. During lunch, Tommy Woodbury offered to share one of his mother's famous chocolate-chip death cookies. Tiffany Washington went out of her way to explain to Molly that the Black Death was a nasty plague that wiped out most of the population of Europe during the 1300's and even wrote down the titles of a few books on the subject that could be found at the library.

Other students commiserated with her, wishing Mr. Robinson was back and dreaming up horrible ways to get rid of the substitute—none of them remotely possible and all of them invoking gales of laughter. Tiffany, still a little miffed at being humiliated in class earlier, wished that a tub of honey would fall on Miss Gordon followed by a vat of fire ants. Molly countered by pointing out that fire ants deserved better and therefore death by guacamole would be more appropriate. Bill Johnson, who was not actually in their class but felt compelled to participate, suggested the substitute be told to copy *"I will not make unreasonable requests of my students that cause them to become apathetic towards the learning process and therefore miss their opportunity at getting into a good college"* ten thousand, two hundred and fifty-seven times on the blackboard. The students exploded into peals of laughter even though most of them didn't know what 'apathetic' meant.

* * * * *

The end of the school day came much too quickly. Molly looked up when the bell rang, dismayed to see that it was already time for class to be dismissed. She had not been able to come up with a suitable reason to refuse her teacher's offer, which meant she would be alone with Miss Gordon once again. Fear and anxiety turned her stomach sour. She touched the amber stone hidden beneath her shirt and suddenly felt calm and sure. All of her apprehension and dread disappeared, replaced by a sense of power. The confidence she felt earlier in the day returned. The Sphinx had indeed given her a powerful amulet.

Miss Gordon finished dismissing the class and returned. She had a look of extreme satisfaction on her face. "Now, Molly, why don't you come to my desk and we can talk about your assignment. Then we'll go over to the computer lab together."

Molly got up from her desk and took a few steps forward, stopping far enough away so that she was out of reach of the teacher. As she waited for the next instruction, she watched Miss Gordon closely and noticed her teacher's eyes starting to change to that peculiar non-color she remembered from before. They widened until they became the focal point in her face and soon Molly found that she could not look away.

"Now, my dear," Miss Gordon said softly as her eyes drilled into Molly, "What have you been up to?"

Molly groped for the topaz pendant and found it just as she began to feel tendrils of the substitute's telepathic control tickling the corners of her mind. As her fingers closed around the talisman, her thoughts instantly cleared. However, she did not make that known. Instead she played along.

"I shared a cookie with Tommy Woodbury at lunch," she replied in a monotone. That was just the sort of thing a girl her age would think was the most important thing in the world. She hoped it was enough to get the crone off her back.

Miss Gordon pursed her lips. "What is this?" She asked in a soothing voice designed to entice answers out of even the most difficult prey. "You have a new plaything around your neck. May I see it?"

Molly panicked for a split second, but the talisman was warm in her fingers and gave her the answer she needed. "Of course, Miss Gordon," she said in a flat voice. She stood up and started to move closer to the desk.

"Take it off, " Miss Gordon said, pointing to the necklace. "Hand it to me. I want a closer look."

Molly stepped up to the desk and began to unclasp the necklace. As she went to take it off, her hand shot out and knocked over a large coffee mug right into the teacher's lap. Miss Gordon gave a startled yelp as she was drenched with cold coffee and her concentration was broken.

"Oh, my goodness!" Molly cried out. "I am soooo sorry! Let me get a towel to clean that up." She backed towards her desk. "I think I saw the janitor a little while ago. He usually has towels and stuff." Before Miss Gordon could protest, Molly grabbed her backpack and ran out of the room. "I'll be right back!" she called over her shoulder as she disappeared through the classroom door.

* * * * *

It took a minute or two before Miss Gordon realized Molly wasn't coming back. She stood up and stormed out of the classroom, coffee still dripping from the front of her white slacks. She wasn't sure exactly what happened, but somehow the girl had been able to break her hold. The child was very lucky—perhaps a little too lucky—which meant there was some kind of magic at work. Ancient and powerful magic, too, since there were few creatures who could counter her own spells. Her eyes narrowed as she thought back to the necklace the girl was clutching so tightly. *Of course. That old fool gave her some kind of protective talisman.* "So you're soliciting help from the old ones, Barnaby," she muttered. "Well, you're not the only one who can call in a favor…" A slow cruel smile started to spread across her chiseled features as she thought of the perfect solution.

CHAPTER 15

Molly was panting and out of breath when she finally made it to Mr. Cotton's front porch. She knocked and then opened the door.

"Come in," he called from the couch in the living room. "You look as if you ran the entire way from school."

"I did," she wheezed. Her lungs hurt and her throat felt as if it was on fire. "Miss Gordon… the necklace…"

"Shhhhh…" he said soothingly, "Relax and catch your breath for a moment. Then you can tell me." He rose from the couch and hobbled into the kitchen. Soon she heard the sound of water running and a clatter of dishes and glassware.

A few minutes later he reappeared, carrying a tray loaded with two tall glasses of iced lemonade and a plate of wedge-shaped shortbread cookies. She gratefully accepted a glass and drank the lemonade down in three gulps.

"Not so fast," he cautioned her. "You'll give yourself a cramp."

She took a deep breath and set the glass down on the coffee table. "Thanks. I feel much better." Now that she was settled, she noticed that her friend was worse than the day before. He looked as if he was aging a little more every day and wore several days' stubble. He appeared gaunt, as if he had not eaten anything since Clarence was taken. His pale complexion only heightened the deep circles under his eyes and his cheeks were hollow. It was apparent sleep was not coming easily. "Mr. Cotton? You don't look so well. Don't you think you should go to the doctor and have them look at your leg? It might be getting infected."

"I'll be okay," he replied quietly. "Besides, there's nothing a doctor can do. It just needs to heal up on its own." He quickly changed the subject. "Now, are you ready to tell me what happened?"

She nodded. "Miss Gordon kept me after school today."

Mr. Cotton frowned. "I was afraid of this. Now that she knows you are close to me, she will try to use you." His face grew more and more solemn as she described the events of the day. But when she got to the part where she tipped the coffee cup into Miss Gordon's lap, he snickered.

"Well, well. I guess you're a little tougher than I supposed," he said with a twinkle in his eye. "But she'll be better prepared next time. It's lucky I asked your mom if you could play hooky from school tomorrow to help me. She said it would be okay this one time."

"You did? Well, I guess I can't turn in any papers tomorrow if I'm not there. And it's Friday too. Maybe by Monday she'll have forgotten or something."

"Yeah… something." He took a coin out of his pocket. Molly was expecting another magic item, so she was a little disappointed to see that it was just an ordinary quarter. It wasn't even a particularly old or special—just a plain boring coin with the familiar dull picture of an eagle on one side and the face of a dead president on the other. He placed it into her palm and closed her fist around it. "No magic here. This quarter is so you can buy yourself a soda at the drugstore."

She bit her lip to keep from laughing. Sodas were a little more than a quarter these days, but she thanked him and added the coin to the stash of change in the front pocket of her jeans. The reality was that a dollar and some change might get her a soda, but she kept that information to herself. She didn't want to insult him.

"Today you'll need to keep your wits about you," he cautioned. "You'll be looking for the Leprechaun and he's quite crafty, especially around money. He would cheat a dying man out of his last red cent if given the chance. He considers all humans to be potential thieves of his treasure, so he's going to be extremely distrustful of you." The old man paused and his expression softened. "However, he's no friend of Miss Gordon and would do anything to see her defeated, even if it meant joining forces with a couple of humans such as you and I."

"What did she do to him?"

"She broke his cauldron and stole his treasure. He got most of his gold back, but Leprechauns have nasty tempers and long memories. He holds a grudge to this day."

He took out another coin from his pocket and turned it over in his fingers. Molly could tell right away that this was not another quarter. It was larger than a half dollar and looked like it was made of gold. It was not quite perfectly round and had strange markings on it like a Spanish doubloon. But this was no doubloon. She was pretty sure she knew exactly what it was even before he handed it to her.

"This is Leprechaun gold, isn't it?"

"Very perceptive of you. This is, in fact, the final coin missing from the Leprechaun's treasure. I want you to return it to him, but be very careful," he warned as he dropped the coin into her waiting hands. "Leprechauns are extremely unpredictable, especially when it comes to their gold, and this one's even worse. You have to be really careful that he doesn't get the idea that you are at all responsible for the burglary. Otherwise, there's no telling what he might do."

"Ummm, so where do I find him?"

"He'll be milling around the drugstore on 32nd Street and Town… close to that new housing development."

Molly grinned. "Oh, I know that place! I go there all the time! I never knew there was a Leprechaun living there…"

"Well there is," Mr. Cotton snapped, "He's been there since before the Wongs bought the place. In fact, Mr. Wong told me once he pays the scoundrel three rolls of quarters and a bottle of Irish whiskey per week for protection." His face turned beet red. "Protection indeed!" he spat. "The only thing the Wongs need protection from is him!"

She waited for him to continue, but it seemed that was the extent of the old man's rant. "Um, okay. So when I get there, how do I find him?"

He took a deep breath and relaxed. "More than likely, the Leprechaun won't approach you, as he doesn't like visitors. He keeps hidden in dark corners—under the cash register and places like that where there's a steady stream of loose change to satisfy some of his cravings." He changed the subject suddenly. "You know, you should really try the peppermint soda from the vending machine at the back of the store—it's really quite refreshing."

"Peppermint soda? I've never heard of that."

He continued as if he hadn't heard her. "After you get the soda, drop the change from the quarter onto the floor and then step back and wait. Maybe that will draw him out long enough for you to give him back the gold." He wagged his finger. "Just make sure you don't give the coin back to that devil until he agrees to help us."

Molly rolled the coin between her thumb and forefinger, examining the strange runes. Then she pocketed it.

Mr. Cotton sat down heavily on the couch. He looked tired, as if the effort of the conversation had drained him. "I can't promise that he will help us at all but he might. At this point even a 'maybe' is worth chasing after." He looked miserable.

I bet he hasn't eaten anything since she kidnapped Clarence, Molly thought. The an idea came to her. "Mr. Cotton," she began carefully. "My mom was wondering if you would like to come to dinner at my house."

"Tonight?"

"Well yeah. Tonight—and maybe for the rest of the week… or until…"

"…Until Clarence comes back."

"Yeah."

He sighed. "Molly, I really appreciate your generosity, but I know how hard things are for your family. I don't want to be an imposition."

"Oh no!" she cried. "You wouldn't be an imposition. It wouldn't be much—we have spaghetti or peanut butter and jelly sandwiches most of the time, but mom is always wishing there were more adults around to talk to."

He smiled. "Well, I have to admit that it has been a little quiet around here—perhaps downright lonely. I would love to have dinner with you and your family one of these nights…" he chuckled, "…Even if it's peanut butter and jelly sandwiches."

She beamed. "Okay, it's settled. I'll ask mom when I get back. Anyway, I better get going if I'm going to get over to the drugstore. My bike has a flat, so I guess I'll be hoofing it."

"Hoofing it?" he asked.

"Walking," she clarified.

He looked a little worried. "Please be careful and keep your eyes about you. Carrying that coin on your person is like having a big neon sign broadcasting your whereabouts. It won't just be Leprechauns that want it. Trolls, Dwarfs, dragons… pretty much any of the creatures that covet treasure can smell Leprechaun gold from miles away."

Molly looked curiously at him. "Why do you still have that coin anyway? Why didn't you give it back to the Leprechaun a long time ago if you've always known where to find him?"

"I didn't steal it," he shot back defensively. "I found it not long after she stole his pot. It must have dropped when she was carrying it off, because it was under a bunch of debris in a gutter pretty far from the drugstore." He looked a little embarrassed. "You're right, I should have returned it long ago. I always meant to, but it's the best thing I've found for baiting dragon traps and almost impossible to come by."

She shook her head. "Dragon traps... Makes perfect sense, I guess."

"Catching dragons just doesn't seem that important right now." He sounded disheartened. "If we don't free Clarence and the others soon, there won't really be a reason to catch dragons... or anything else for that matter."

Molly silently agreed. Already two days had gone by. They were running out of time.

CHAPTER 16

Twenty minutes later, Molly strolled past the city park. It was a pleasantly warm afternoon and the air was heavily scented with late spring flowers such as jasmine, honeysuckle and roses. Sparrows argued in the trees above her, chasing one another over a common love interest. She was starting to let her mind wander when she heard a sneeze close by. She looked around but saw nothing but a large lilac bush. The bush sneezed again.

"Psssd. Diddo girl. Cub here." The voice came from the bush. "You're Bolly, ride?"

She stopped in her tracks and nodded, but didn't approach any closer. She remembered Mr. Cotton's warning about carrying Leprechaun gold. "I hab a bessage for you," the voice snuffled. "frub a fred."

She frowned and stood her ground. "What friend?" she asked suspiciously, crossing her arms over her chest in a defiant manner.

"He said his dabe bas Barcus," the voice replied. There was another loud sneeze, this time strong enough to rock the lilac bush and send a bunch of tiny purple flowers into the air.

"Marcus," She repeated the name slowly, pretending she didn't recognize it. In reality, the possibility that this was a message from the winged horse thrilled her. She paused, waiting for further explanation. After a moment she became impatient. "Well, what did Marcus say?"

The voice from the bush sniffled and then replied peevishly, "Dook, diddo girl, I didit wot to sid oud id dis stupid bush—I'b horribly allergic to... ah... plads. Bud he idsisded. He wadded be to tell you to be careful. You're beebing hudded by a tody-gazer." "A what?" she asked. She had never heard the term before. "A tody-gazer," the voice sighed in exasperation. "You dow, basilisks, cockatrices... tody-gazers."

She frowned as she tried to figure out what the voice was saying. "A toady-gazer?" Mr. Cotton had a basilisk but it never gazed at toads...

"Ugh!" the voice exclaimed. "Stupid girl! Barcus tode me you were sbard and wise. He doesid dow bud he's dalkig aboud." It sneezed again and several glossy green leaves flew past where Molly was standing. "to-dey-ga-zer." It tried again. "You dow, thigs thad turd you to stode if you dook id der eyes. Surely you dow about deb."

"Oh, right. Stoney-gazer. I get it now," she replied, feeling a little embarrassed. She looked around but didn't see anything following her that might fit the description. "Where?" she asked the voice.

"You cad't see deb, bud dey're really close," the voice warned. "You should keep your wids about you." It erupted into a fit of sneezing.

There was a terrible crash and then another a loud sneeze and a pop. Wispy tendrils of pink smoke floated out from the lilac bush.

Molly stood there for a moment wondering just what had happened. *A spy?* Not likely. Marcus was gone before Miss Gordon attacked Mr. Cotton's house and there was little chance that the monster would have known the extent of their friendship. She thought about searching for some trace of whatever had spoken to her, but soon decided against it. There was still a chance that this was a trap. *A trap... what if?* A sudden disturbing thought surfaced and she thrust her hand onto her front pocket to make sure the Leprechaun's gold was still there. Feeling the coin's cool surface against her fingers gave her a sense of relief. *Well, at least the thing in the bush wasn't a magic pickpocket,* she sighed. She started walking again with a new sense of urgency. There were only a few blocks left to go and who knew what else she might run into on the way.

CHAPTER 17

The store was a tiny hole-in-the-wall, completely invisible save for the words *"Don's Drugstore"* lettered in faded red paint on the dirty front windows. Molly's arrival was heralded by a jingle from a string of tiny brass bells attached to the door. She walked in and waved to the elderly man behind the counter. "Hi, Mr. Wong."

The shopkeeper looked up from his newspaper and grinned at her, displaying his three remaining front teeth. He pointed to a hand-lettered sign that read, *'Please Check all Bags.'* She showed him her empty hands and made a pirouette to show him she wasn't wearing a backpack. He nodded and went back to reading.

The store was cluttered with all matter of sundries, from stale cough drops to sunglasses. Molly loved the place because it reminded her of the family run grocery stores on the islands. It even smelled like the stores back home—the aroma of coconut air fresheners competing with chow mein noodles. Remembering Mr. Cotton's instructions, she sought out something dispensing peppermint soda. She wasn't too hopeful, since she was pretty familiar with the store and didn't recall ever seeing any vending machines before. After treading carefully through an aisle cluttered with toothpaste, Christmas decorations, anchovies, toy dinosaurs and strange candy with edible rice paper wrappers, she stumbled across a rusty-looking vending machine tucked in the back of the store, partially obscured by some lawn chairs and a five gallon bucket jammed with vinyl umbrellas. Her mouth dropped open in astonishment. *Why didn't I notice this before?*

Moving the bucket a few feet away, she noticed the soda machine bore faded paper labels with photographs of old fashioned cans. There was a round button and a small light next to each label. Most of the lights were lit, indicating they were out of stock. However, there seemed to still be at least one can of peppermint soda since that light was still off. *Not a very popular flavor*, she thought. She noticed the faded price next to the picture. *Fifteen cents? Is that for real?* The old man had been right about one thing—a quarter would get her a soda and change.

Although it looked like one of those money-eating monsters, she thought she might as well take a chance and buy a soda from the machine. The worst thing that could happen was that it would jam and she would be out a quarter. It was a risk she could live with. She pulled the quarter out of her pocket and dropped it into the machine.

It banged around a little until it fell into the change box with a clink. She waited a moment, then pushed the button next to the picture of the peppermint soda can and waited. At first nothing happened, so she pushed the button again a little harder.

There was a clatter as a can of soda was released from somewhere deep inside. It rattled around for a few moments and then appeared at the opening in the bottom of the machine. She retrieved the can and was just about to open it when she caught a movement out of the corner of her eye. It might have been a large cat or a small dog… or perhaps something else completely. She purposely left the dime in the coin return. Grabbing the closest lawn chair, she moved it behind a rack of sunglasses in order to have an unobstructed view of the machine while simultaneously concealing herself. Then she sat down to wait.

She didn't have to wait very long. After a few moments, there was a funny scrabbling sound from behind the vending machine. Then a rather grubby-looking little man dressed in shorts and a t-shirt darted forward and snatched the dime. Holding it up triumphantly, he squealed, "Aha! I got it!"

Molly suspected this must be the Leprechaun because he wore funny elf-like shoes with large silver buckles and green and red striped tights. He also had a mop of carrot-colored hair and a scraggly beard, both in bad need of a trim. "Excuse me," she addressed him as politely as she could without giggling. "I believe that's my change."

He blinked at her in surprise but almost immediately regained his composure. "And what would you be bringin' me in return for this wee bit o' treasure?"

"Oh, for Pete's sake, it's only a dime," she grumbled, but then remembered she was here to ask a favor. She gave him the sweetest smile she good muster. "You're a Leprechaun, aren't you?"

The tiny man looked at her suspiciously. "Me? Oh no, Lass, Not I! A Leprechaun, you say? Around these parts? I don't know what you're talking about." He sized her up and sniffed. "Hmmm… you've the Sight, that's for sure. And by the smell o' ye, you've got something else as well." He sniffed again. "*Me gold!* You've got me gold in your pocket!"

She pulled the piece of gold from her pocket and held it out to him. But before he could snatch it from her fingers, she thrust her arm high in the air so the coin was out of his reach. He hopped up and down furiously, but couldn't reach her outstretched arm.

"This gold?" she asked innocently. "Oh no, this gold can't possibly be yours. You see, it belongs to a Leprechaun and I'm supposed to give it only to him." She smiled innocently. "Are you absolutely sure you haven't seen one? I was told he usually hangs around this store."

He shifted his weight uncomfortably. "Aye, Lass, maybe I've seen him," he admitted.

Molly started to put the coin back in her pocket.

"Wait! No, don't do that," he protested. "All right. I know where the Leprechaun is. Give me the gold and I'll make sure he gets it." He held out his hand and waited expectantly, drumming a foot on the ground like an impatient rabbit.

"Not so fast. I need to talk to him first. I need his help."

He sighed and put his hand down. "Fine. You've got me. I'm t' one you're looking for." He bowed. "Sean Cornelius O'Brien de Cervantes at your service. Now give me back me gold."

"De Cervantes?" Molly sounded unconvinced. "That doesn't sound very Irish to me…"

The Leprechaun looked uncomfortable. "Black Irish. On me pappy's side," he admitted. "Me great-grandmother married a Spaniard. They say he washed up on t' beach after the English defeated the Armada."

She gave him a clumsy little curtsy. "Nice to meet you, Mr. O'Brien de Cervantes." She stumbled a little on the long name.

He doubled over with laughter. "Oh my! Mr. O'Brien de Cervantes. That's indeed a mouthful, Lass. Just call me 'Cornelius' Never cared much for Sean. T'was the name of me sister's first beau, and oh how we all despised him…" he caught himself and changed the subject. "Enough about me family. Who might you be?" he asked.

"I'm Molly… Molly Stevens," she stammered. "Mr. Cotton, my next door neighbor, sent me to find you and give you this coin. He said he found it after the witch came and stole your gold."

Cornelius looked at her with a mixture of curiosity and distrust. He frowned and shook his head. "He told you she's a witch?" he asked.

"Well… not exactly," she answered a little sheepishly. "He actually never told me what she is. I sort of assumed she must be a witch. I mean she kind of looks like one and most definitely acts like one."

He threw back his head and laughed. "Oh my! A witch!" he roared. "You figgered she's a witch!" He wiped a tear from one of his bright blue eyes. "Just how many witches have you made acquaintances with t' prompt ye t' make that assessment, Lass?"

"Ummm… just her," Molly squeaked nervously.

"Well, you'd be dead wrong. That un's most definitely not a witch. Witches are humans who've learned Faerie Ways and who might have a touch o' the Sight., like you—though I don't think you've learned anything yet. Do you know how t' sour cow's milk or strike a wheat field with ergot?" He peered at her, daring her to answer him.

"Don't need to," she fired back. "There aren't any cows in the city and the climate's all wrong for growing wheat."

"Details," he grumbled. "Well, that un's no witch. She eats witches like you for lunch. You'd be wise t' steer clear o' her completely. That's the best advice I can give ye."

"It's too late for that," Molly whimpered. "I can't 'steer clear' of her. She's my school teacher." She briefly told him the story.

When she was finished the Leprechaun looked grim and shook his head. "This is bad business… very bad business. I'm not fond o' Griffins, but even one o' those thievin' gold hoarders don't deserve what she'll do t' him." He paused. "You really don't have much o' a chance o' savin' him… unless…" He looked up at her with a strange gleam in his eyes. "You said you have already sought out the Sphinx, and he gave you a talisman."

She nodded and pulled it out of her shirt. The golden topaz sparkled in the dim light.

"I see the Sphinx found you strong o' heart. That's promising. Now you'll also need t' be like quicksilver in both mind and body." He lifted one eyebrow. "What do I mean by this?" he asked.

"Quicksilver… Ummmm…" She thought about it for a moment, and then brightened. "Quicksilver is another name for mercury, which is a metal but behaves like a liquid. It never dissolves or mixes with anything because it's an element."

"Exactly. Go on…"

She frowned and thought hard. "So… What you are saying is that I need to be adaptable, but still be myself and not let myself turn into something else."

"Well, by me uncle's last shamrock," he laughed. "That's a deep and thought-provoking thing to come from such a young 'un."

She was puzzled. "Wasn't that what you were looking for?"

"No, but it's a hopping good answer. I wouldn't ha' thought o' that myself. You're a smart lass."

"So I've passed your test and proven myself?"

"Not exactly," he replied with an odd little twinkle lighting up his blue eyes. "But now I know you're smart enough t' be put t' the test. Now, before we get started," his tone grew serious. "I think we've established that I'm the Leprechaun you be looking for—which means I'm entitled t' the return o' that gold coin in your pocket." There was something hungry about his expression as he stared at her with anticipation.

She groaned and withdrew the coin. His reasoning was sound—after all, she had told him she was here to return the treasure to its rightful owner... And he was the rightful owner. But she had hoped to get his promise to help her as part of the deal. Instead, all she had was the assertion from Cornelius that she still needed to prove herself before he would consent to help her. She felt a little cheated, but still handed over the gold to him without argument.

He ran the coin through his fingers again and again, sighing with pleasure. Molly thought he looked a lot like her little brother Dylan, who wore the same ecstatic look when he had his thumb stuck in his mouth and his nose buried in his blankie. She fought back a giggle. Her mouth was dry and she remembered the peppermint soda. She grabbed the old-fashioned ring tab and pulled.

There was a hiss followed by a spray of foam as the soda exploded in her hands. She instinctively put her lips on the can to suck up the foam before it dripped everywhere, and was pleasantly surprised by the taste. The idea of peppermint soda seemed gross, sort of like fizzy toothpaste, but it was clear and refreshing—not too sweet or too minty. She gulped down the contents of the can as if she were dying of thirst.

"Don't slurp!" the Leprechaun sniggered. "That's strong stuff you're drinking there. It'll put hair on your chest."

Molly looked down in horror for a brief second before realizing the Leprechaun was joking.

"Okay enough kidding around. Ye still have t' prove yourself." He walked around her in deep concentration. "Ummmm… let me see…" He looked up at a nonexistent point near the ceiling. "What can I make ye do?"

"Don't you already have some standard test you give people? Like a riddle or something?"

The Leprechaun looked at her with annoyance. "What d' ye think I am? Some old goat put here on this earth t' test the wit o' some young 'un who brings me back me rightful property?" he scoffed. "I didn't know ye'd be coming, so I've got t' think of something." He sounded a little defensive. "Besides," he growled, "I'da thought the Sphinx might have told ye how stupid riddles are. It's a pet peeve o' his."

"Yeah, he sort of mentioned something like that," she admitted.

Cornelius paced back and forth, scratching his thin, scraggly, ginger-colored beard. "Now if I know that Sphinx, he'd a let ye off easy. Let me guess, he probably didn't even give ye a real test…" He peered sideways at her. "In fact, I'd wager he just asked ye t' pick some posies from his little garden."

She flushed with embarrassment.

"Thought so. That Sphinx has always had a soft spot for young 'uns, especially lasses." He paused and looked at the piece of gold in his hand. "Wait, I've got it!" Stepping up close to her, he poked her kneecap. "I've got a challenge that'll prove how smart ye *really* are."

Molly was a little nervous now. The Leprechaun was smiling, but it was not a friendly grin. His face was cold and his eyes gleamed like pieces of blue ice. He walked around her sizing her up once more, as if he wanted a last look before he sent her to her doom.

He cleared his throat and puffed up like a self-important rooster. "Not far from here," he began dramatically, "there be a small village behind a great wall. Once upon a time it was chock full o' folks like yourself, but over time they all moved away and now the whole town is silent and empty."

She wracked her mind trying to think where she might have seen an empty village but couldn't think of anything that fit that description. "Why'd they move?"

"Now does that really matter, lass?"

"I guess not... unless they moved because of an earthquake or a natural disaster." She shifted her weight uncomfortably from side to side.

"Well, they didn't," he snapped. "Nobody really knows why they left." His eyes darkened and glittered like cold sapphires at midnight. "Deep in the village, there be a particular house where me treasure is hidden. Go get it and bring it back t' me. Then I'll know you'll be worthy o' me help."

"But I already gave you the coin," she argued. "You were supposed to help me. Mr. Cotton said you would."

"Are ye too frightened to even try, lass?" Cornelius sneered. "Would ye rather go home and tell Mr. Cotton that ye returned me treasure and then ran off like a scared rabbit when I'd be willing t' help ye? Oh, I'm sure he'd like t' hear that." He threw his head back and roared with laughter. Then just as suddenly, he was serious again and his voice became a icy whisper that sent shivers down Molly's spine, "Or perhaps you'd prefer t' face yer '*witch*' without me help."

She trembled and shook her head. "I am not afraid of your silly little test," she lied. "I'll go."

A smile slowly spread across the Leprechaun's face. "Good. You'll need t' go quickly, before it gets dark. T'would be bad business if you're still inside the village gates once the sun sets." He pulled out a tattered scrap of paper with something written in childish script. "Here's the address," he said as he thrust the paper into her hand.

She turned it over. On the back there was a crudely drawn map. She recognized the place now. *Village indeed*, she thought. It was an empty housing tract only a few blocks away. The 'X' that marked the house was in the middle of a meandering labyrinth of circular streets and dead ends. Molly sighed and resigned herself to the fact that it was going to be a long walk. "Okay, what am I looking for, anyway?" she asked a little peevishly.

"A toy lockbox—the kind that wee 'uns keep their pennies and bottle caps in."

"That's a weird place to store gold," she observed. "Why don't you keep it in a safe or something."

The Leprechaun scowled. "That's none o' your minding," he snapped. "You jus' get the box and bring it back here." He rummaged through the contents of a shelf marked '*Clearance*' until he found a small penlight attached to a keychain. It was a noxious shade of bright pink with lavender ponies painted on its handle. "Here, ye might need this once you're inside..." He murmured as he handed it to her.

Molly tried not to grimace as she took the flashlight and tucked it away in her backpack.

"Now keep your wits about you and get in and out as fast as you can," he advised in a hushed voice. "And watch yer back. They hunt in packs."

She frowned. "Should I be expecting to meet up with a pack of wild dogs or something?"

"Not dogs..." he added evasively and didn't elaborate. However, his shifting gaze and nervous demeanor betrayed his fear.

Not dogs, Molly thought as she watched the play of emotions across his face. Whatever was out there scared the Leprechaun enough to not want to venture close, even to retrieve his own gold. It puzzled her. She ran down a mental list of wild animals that could be hiding in an empty housing tract until one came to mind: a coyote. *It had to be coyotes*, she decided, remembering a recent news story about one of the wild canines carrying off a small child. She supposed the Leprechaun had good reason to fear coyotes. He really wasn't much taller than her three-year-old brother. She, on the other hand, was too big to be carried off and therefore didn't fear the scrappy animals. Her courage returned.

Cornelius noticed her change of heart and smiled crookedly. He pulled out a pocket watch from somewhere in his clothing and consulted it. "Ye don't have much time, so ye better be off. I'll be waiting over there when ye get back." He nodded towards the vending machine. "By the way, the store closes at seven... sharp. That leaves ye 'round about two hours to get back here."

"What if I'm late?"

"Tardiness will not be tolerated," the Leprechaun said in an almost perfect mimic of Miss Gordon's high-pitched voice. Then with a loud pop he disappeared into thin air.

Molly shuddered. Even though she knew it was just an imitation, the familiar voice gave her goose bumps. She crushed the empty soda can with her heel and picked it up to deposit into the recycle bin near the front entrance of the store. On her way out she paused long enough to buy an Almond Joy and three Slim Jims from the wizened man behind the counter. He rung her up and then handed her a fourth.

"For your friend," he whispered.

She started to ask him what he was talking about but he put a finger to his lips and nodded towards the aisle where the vending machine stood at attention.

Molly nodded in understanding, although she secretly thought the old man must be mistaken. The Leprechaun was not her friend, nor did she believe he would consume something as overly processed, chemically laden and delicious as a Slim Jim. *If he ate anything* (and she pondered this for a moment before deciding he must), *it would have to be something magical, like beer brewed in eggshells or something gross like that.* She retrieved her change and shoved the pepperoni sticks into her backpack. The Almond Joy she hung on to, intending to eat it as soon as she got outside.

The bells fastened to the door tinkled a random melody as she opened the shop door and left the store. She eyed the sky as she waited for the traffic signal to turn. The sun was pretty low and she needed to hurry. There was maybe another hour of daylight and she figured it would take at least twenty minutes to get to the house where the Leprechaun's treasure was stashed, She was just crossing the street when she heard the jangle of bells again. She turned and looked back at the store, but the sidewalk was empty. Shrugging, she pressed on.

CHAPTER 18

J ust past an empty strip mall and across the street from a
small neighborhood of older ranch style houses sprawled
out comfortably on half-acre lots, the tightly packed development of brand new homes seemed out of place. The twen-
ty-foot wall surrounding the gated community made it resemble
some kind of medieval village, complete with decorative struc-
tures every hundred feet that looked like turrets. Molly half-ex-
pected to see the towers of a real castle rising above the houses,
but instead all she saw was row after row of terra cotta tiled roofs
disappearing into the hills. *There must be hundreds. How will I ever find
the right one?* She pulled out the map. From what she could make
out, it was a much more simplified rendition of the maze in front
of her. She groaned and looked at her watch. She'd be lucky if
she could get to the address and back to the store before closing.

She turned down the street that marked the beginning of
the abandoned development and saw an empty guardhouse. A
crooked real-estate sign stood like a silent sentinel next to the
weed-choked building. The builders had gone out of business
before the project was complete and now the entire thing was for
sale—all 142 acres of prime residentially-zoned property.

As she eased herself under the barricade she heard a rustle
behind her. She paused and waited for the sound to repeat itself
but all was quiet except the hum of the cars on the interstate
behind her. There weren't even any birds. She raised one eyebrow
in perplexity and slowly turned around, only to find nothing

behind her but a withered box hedge. She took a Slim Jim out of her pocket and unwrapped it. *Maybe it's just a hungry stray dog or cat,* she thought as she broke off a piece and placed it carefully on the step of the guardhouse. At least she hoped it was a stray dog or cat… or some other creature that would find pepperoni sticks more appetizing than little girls.

After a several minutes of inactivity from the bush, she figured the sound was just a bird or a rabbit settling itself. She passed a second wooden barricade with peeling white paint, fastened with a chain and padlock to block the road from unwanted visitors. She walked away, glancing over her shoulder every few minutes to see if anything investigated the snack she left, but the Slim Jim was still untouched when the guardhouse finally disappeared from view.

It was eerie walking alone through the unfinished neighborhood. Tumbleweeds gathered on porches against doors of incomplete houses. Dirt and debris littered empty streets that had never been driven on. Every once in a while she recognized the distinctive messy tangles of a black widow web at the entrance to a darkened basement window. The webs were a grim reminder that there was nobody around to keep out the native fauna, some of which might be dangerous. Molly made a mental note to watch her step when she went inside. Spiders didn't scare her but the idea of running across a rattlesnake did.

She realized with a start that she no longer heard any of the normal sounds she was accustomed to. All she heard was the wind howling as it whipped around the empty buildings. A tumbleweed rolled past at a fast clip, narrowly missing her. It continued down the road until it slammed into several others piled high against the doors to a community center.

Brushing an unruly lock of hair out of her face, Molly pulled the map from her pocket. The street she was looking for was around the next bend. As she turned the paper over to reread the address, it was snatched out of her fingers by the strong wind. It rose high in the air, lifted up by the breeze until it was higher than the rooftops. She watched it roll and tumble in the air until it sailed over the grey tile roof of a three-story house and was gone. Panic sent a lump into her throat as a horrible thought materialized. *How am I going to find my way home?* Without the map, she wasn't sure if she'd be able to remember the way through the circular maze of streets and dead ends. She paused, wondering if she should turn back. *No,* she decided. *I've gotten this far. I might as well get the Leprechaun's box and then figure out how to get out of here How hard can it be?*

"28675 Rosewood Lane… 28675 Rosewood Lane…" she chanted to herself under her breath to remember the address. It became her mantra as she continued along the cracked sidewalk. She rounded the corner and saw a signpost: *Rosewood Lane.* A yellow sign warned that there was no outlet. *This is definitely the place,* she thought as she crossed the street and headed into the cul de sac.

The road wound upwards into the hills at the back of the development. Unlike the smaller homes on the main road, the mini-mansions she now passed were set a little way back from the street, with wide circular driveways and larger lots. But even these expansive lawns were brown; the tropical landscaping blackened and dead. She noticed the way the desert was starting to creep back. But still there were no birds or other sounds. *There should at least be birds,* she thought with a shiver. There was definitely something not right about this place. But it was too late to go back.

"28675," she said out loud. Her voice sounded loud and unfamiliar in the silent neighborhood. The sun was now quite low in the sky and cast long shadows as twilight approached. Molly consulted her watch and realized that she had less than an hour and a half before nightfall—even less if she was going to make it back before the store closed its doors for the night. She was thankful for the flashlight. Already she could see through the windows of the houses that the interiors were pitch black.

"28879…28791…"

The end of the street came into view as did the address she was looking for. Molly froze. She now knew what the Leprechaun feared and why he had sent her instead of retrieving his treasure himself.

CHAPTER 19

The house was constructed to look like an old fashioned Spanish hacienda with white stucco and a red terra cotta roof. A high wall surrounded what must have been intended to be a beautiful courtyard with a Mediterranean garden. Bougainvillea grew untamed over the front porch, almost concealing it completely with a cascade of orange flowers. However, it wasn't the house or the garden that had caught Molly's attention and made her stop in her tracks. It was the massive cougar-sized feline sitting on top of the wall.

She gasped and stood very still, hoping at first that the creature might not have seen her and then realizing that this was improbable, since it stared at her with a curious look. Its mouth and most of its face were human, but its eyes and nose were those of a large cat. From its size and thick beard she could tell it was a full grown male. At her approach, in scorpion fashion, he raised a tail tipped with bristling sharp needles like a porcupine.

A manticore.

Goosebumps erupted up and down her arms and she prayed he wasn't hungry. Fear gripped her like a vice around her throat as she remembered what Mr. Cotton had told her when she first saw the manticore cub in his shed.

"*...they always travel in prides—like lions...*"

She wanted very badly to look around to see where the others might be hiding, but she dared not take her eyes off the beast on the wall. He lowered his tail but continued to train his great green lamppost eyes on her. She slowly and carefully moved one hand to the pocket where she kept the Slim Jims. It was a small chance, but perhaps the beast might have a taste for them.

The creature stiffened slightly, but didn't make any move to attack. Instead he extended one claw and used it as a toothpick to dislodge a morsel that was stuck between his teeth. He caught the offending piece of food and examined it for a moment before deftly flicking it away.

"Poor little kitten," he remarked, not aware that she could understand him. "You probably think you're looking at a mangy bobcat. I bet you're wondering if I'm big enough to jump on you and tear your throat out." He appeared to be ignoring her, but she suspected this was a ruse. "Ahhhhh," he sighed and lowered his tail. "It's been a long time since I've tasted a child's scent on the wind. You smell so young and tender... And deliciously afraid. If only I hadn't gorged myself earlier..."

Molly showed no sign that she heard anything he said or that she recognized him for anything more than a regular wild cat. Instead she lowered her hand and murmured, "Nice kitty... stay right there kitty..." She wondered if he could control his appearance through glamour like the Sphinx, or if he was more like Clarence and just appeared in whatever form was most acceptable to humans. She suspected the latter, but didn't want to take any chances that he might disappear.

"Nice kitty indeed," the manticore snorted. "You are indeed a stupid kitten, addressing me like some kind of common pet." He sniffed the air. "Where did you come from anyway? Humans almost never come here anymore and there is an odd scent about you." He stood up and stretched. "No matter. You won't get far. We'll let the cubs hunt you down once it gets dark. That'll be good sport for them. Until then, I'll just let you think you're escaping." He jumped off the wall, disappearing from sight on the other side.

Molly waited a couple of minutes, not daring to move lest the creature suddenly reappear. A rustle from somewhere behind her startled her. *One of the cubs?* She wheeled around, but saw nothing in the fading light. Pulling out a pepperoni stick, she unwrapped it and threw it in the direction of the noise, hoping that whatever it was would pause long enough to investigate the snack and allow her time to get a nice head start.

She heard voices from the direction of the backyard where the manticore disappeared. Molly recognized the deep baritone of the manticore, but couldn't make out what was being said. She didn't have much of a chance against one manticore—let alone an entire pride of them—but she knew she was a sitting duck if she stayed where she was.

Out of the corner of her eye, she noticed a broken basement window. It looked big enough to squeeze through but too small for the large manticore to follow. Of course a cub would have no trouble following her through the window, but hopefully getting out of the open would slow her pursuers long enough for her to find a suitable and more secure hiding place. She dashed across the lawn and carefully eased herself through the opening. Once inside she turned and looked back towards where the Slim Jim had landed. It was gone.

CHAPTER 20

The basement was pitch black. Molly fumbled until she located the flashlight and flicked it on. The disappointingly dim circle of light it cast illuminated a small room with a few dusty boxes strung with cobwebs. She sighed and relaxed. No rattlesnakes. But her relief was short-lived. There was nowhere to hide, nor was it possible to seal the opening. She stacked several of the smaller boxes against the window. They wouldn't hold anything out for long but she hoped they would at least slow the manticores a little once they began their pursuit. She looked around for a way out and spotted a staircase at the far end of the room. *Please, don't let it be locked.*

Luck was with her and the door opened easily. She peered around the corner and found herself in an expansive pantry just off the kitchen. She held her breath and listened. Everything was quiet, so she tiptoed out into the kitchen. There was still enough daylight shining through the boarded up French doors to provide a little illumination. She carefully peeked through a small opening between two pieces of plywood and saw a large backyard with a green mossy pool ringed by giant manmade stones. The manticore pride had settled here where presumably they had access to water. In addition to the large male she encountered earlier, there were three females and several cubs. The remains of two shredded bedrolls and a couple of backpacks lay discarded a little ways from the group, between another outcrop of rocks. Molly was pretty sure that the unlucky owners of the camping gear never left the backyard. She didn't see them but the large cloud of flies buzzing over something concealed behind a large stone told a gruesome story.

Every so often one of the beasts glanced over towards the house as if aware of her presence. The cubs seemed particularly excited and kept wandering towards the house, only to be called back by one of the adults. The pride was apparently content to let the Molly explore the house undisturbed. It would be quite another matter in a few hours when darkness fell and the hunt began.

She turned her attention back to her plight. She needed a secure place to hide until she could reach Mr. Cotton. He would know what to do. At the thought of her friend a lump rose in her throat and she fought back the tears that started to bead in her eyes. *Not now,* she told herself. *I have to stay calm.* The open layout of the home's lower floor was not going to help her, so she climbed the spiral staircase to the second floor.

Molly peeked into each of the bedrooms in turn. She saw a few leaves and some debris strewn over the dirty carpet, but little else that might help her. The small closets were windowless spaces with sliding panel doors that would provide no protection or chance of escape. A tear ran down her cheek as she became more and more desperate. But when she entered the walk-in closet in the master bedroom, she spotted her salvation in the form of a trapdoor in the ceiling. By hopping as high as she could, she managed to grab the rope handle and pulled down the trapdoor. As it opened, a ladder unfolded from inside and extended smoothly to the ground. Climbing up, she found herself in a hot stuffy crawl space. She shined her flashlight around to see if there were any other openings, but aside from a vent housing a large attic fan, the crawl space was self-contained. The only way in or out was through the trapdoor, which she could pull up behind her and tuck the rope up inside.

She was tempted to pull the ladder up behind her at that very moment, but then she remembered the Leprechaun's request of her and she decided to go back down. *After all,* she told herself, *if I am going to come all this way and risk my life, at least I can get what I came here for.* A quick glance through the large window in the master bedroom showed her that the manticores were still all napping by the pool.

As she explored each room in turn, she began to wonder if the treasure was even in the house at all. There were no secret panels, no trapdoors carefully hidden beneath carpet, no secret cubbies in walls. Each room was completely bare and devoid of anything suitable for hiding treasure. She was about to give up when she noticed a broken dresser partially hidden behind the closet door in the last bedroom. She carefully pulled out the empty drawers to reveal a cavity behind the dresser. Hidden in the farthest corner was a small object wrapped in a dirty piece of curtain torn away from one of the windows. She unwrapped it and turned the lockbox over in her hands. Although it was made of metal, it was strangely light. She slid open the lock and looked inside, only to find the box empty.

Her heart sank. Someone had gotten here first and taken the treasure. Now there was no way to get the Leprechaun to help her, even if she was able to get back. She turned the lockbox over and over in her hands in despair. *No… no… no… This can't be happening! What am I going to do?* She opened the box again and almost dropped it in surprise—it was now filled to the brim with golden coins identical to the one she had given back to Cornelius. *Of course.* The box was enchanted so that anyone opening it would think it was empty. Turning the box over must have dispelled the magic. But now that she had the gold, there was still the slight problem of getting it back to the Leprechaun.

She was just considering this when a large crash startled her. It could only mean one thing. She hurried back down the hall to the master bedroom and looked out the window. The backyard was empty. Her time was up. She heard another crash—this time closer—accompanied by the sound of clawed feet scrabbling on the tile floors.

"Come out come out, wherever you are…" the voice sounded like a small boy. Molly suspected it was one of the manticore cubs.

Another juvenile voice snapped, "Shhhhh! You're not supposed to talk to the prey…"

"It's just a human. They can't hear us anyway," the first cub whined.

"Humans can hear us. They just can't understand our speech. It'll still know you're here."

"Ha! It'll know we're here because you're a clumsy oaf and broke that mirror…"

"You pushed me!"

"Quiet! Both of you," a deep voice growled. Molly recognized it as the male she saw earlier. "What have I told you about hunting humans? No talking!"

Terror turned her blood to ice. She dashed into the closet and hurried up the ladder. As she pulled it up behind her, she heard the beasts reach the second floor.

Only now did it occur to her that the rope was still on the outside. Slowly she eased the door open a crack and reached her hand out to retrieve the rope. There was a loud crack as the door to the master bedroom splintered, accompanied by a yelp from one of the cubs. Molly closed her fingers around the rope and pulled it inside just as the first of the creatures found the closet door.

There was a snarl from the adult and a thump as he leapt up. He tried a second time and the trapdoor creaked and opened a tiny bit from the impact. Molly realized it wouldn't take much for the creature to hook a claw inside and pull the whole thing down. She quickly scanned the attic for something she could use to keep the trapdoor shut. Finding a board, she wedged it under the ladder so that it barricaded the door. She hid in the farthest corner of the attic and listened to the sounds of the beasts hunting her. It sounded as if they were tearing the closet apart looking for another way up to the attic. She hoped they didn't think to come in through the roof. She wasn't sure how secure the vent would be against them. Reaching into her pocket, she drew out the vial containing Marcus's hair and shook it out until it lay on her palm like a piece of silver thread. "Oh, Marcus," she whimpered, closing her fingers around the hair. "Will I see anyone ever again?"

Night fell and wrapped everything up in darkness. The manticores grew tired of the hunt and left the house to return to their places by the pool. By turning her head just a little, Molly could just make out a single star through the space between the grates in the attic vent. She watched it twinkle until she fell into a troubled sleep.

CHAPTER 21

olly woke to the sound of pounding on the trapdoor and a familiar voice calling her name. "Molly! Are you in there?" It was Mr. Cotton.

She stretched and groaned. Moonlight streamed in from the attic vent, indicating that some time had passed and the moon was now high in the sky. Suddenly she remembered where she was and panic set in. She stood up and banged her head against the low ceiling. "Ow!" she cried out, more in surprise than pain. She rubbed her head where a small knot was already beginning to form.

The knocking sounded again. "Molly! Is that you?"

"I'm here!" she called as she worked to remove the board from the ladder. With a little effort, she was able to free it and push the trapdoor open a crack. She saw the top of Mr. Cotton's head. "I'm so glad to see you!" she exclaimed.

He clasped her extended hand and gave it a reassuring squeeze. "I am so relieved to find you unharmed," he sighed.

"But what about the…"

"You're safe for now… The manticores won't bother you anymore." He had a queer tone to his voice.

"What? How?"

"I can't explain it. In fact, I was hoping you had an answer." He grabbed the rope and pulled the ladder all the way down. "You should come out. I really don't think we should linger here."

She was alarmed by the sound of his voice. He was nervous and on edge. She quickly descended. The moonlight streamed through the dirty curtains and cast a blue light over everything. It made her friend look ghostly pale, accentuating the dark circles under his eyes and the hollowed cheeks. He was hunched over as if he had aged twenty years in the span of a few hours. His leg was still bandaged and he supported himself with a crutch. She looked back at the trapdoor in the ceiling and noticed large scratch marks deeply embedded in the wood and shivered.

"You were very lucky to find that hiding place. And very resourceful too, I might add," he observed. "Calling Marcus like that."

"I did what?"

"You summoned Marcus with that tail hair of his. Smart girl. When he realized where you were, he came to me straight away." He motioned towards the door. "He's waiting outside to take us both home."

She followed him out of the closet.

When they were on the stairs he turned on her. "What on earth did that beastly Leprechaun think he was going to accomplish, sending you out into manticore territory like that?" His face flushed red with anger. "He might have well just trussed you up like a holiday turkey, stuck an apple in your mouth and left you on their doorstep. And another thing…" he raged as he descended the stairs. "Why didn't you tell me where you were going? Do you have any idea how much danger you were in? I have no idea how you managed to get past Primus and get inside the house in the first place!"

"He… the manticore… I mean the big male one… is that Primus? Well, he let me go past him. He said he was too full to chase me down quite yet."

Mr. Cotton stopped in his tracks and looked at her. "He spoke to you?" he asked astonished. "And you lived to tell me? Nobody ever speaks to a manticore."

"Well he didn't really talk to me… he sort of talked at me," she explained. "He didn't know I could see him. He thought I was seeing a bobcat."

"You're exactly right. If he had any inkling you could see his true form or understand his speech, we wouldn't be having this conversation. He'd never have told you anything. Nor would he ever let you out of his sight. He'd just have poisoned you right there and saved you for later. No, you were very wise to stay quiet and pretend not to see him. That took a lot of courage."

She nodded, pale and frightened. The magnitude of what might have happened was beginning to set in. "Where are the manticores now?" she asked. "What happened? How were you able to get past them?"

"You don't know?" He looked perplexed. "Come on. There's something I think you need to see." He extended his hand out to her.

Together they continued down the staircase. There were more manticore tracks on the stairs, obscuring the distinctive prints of Molly's sneakers. She only now realized how clear her trail was and how silly it was to think she could hide from them. *If I had tried to hide anywhere else…* She shook her head to ward off that vision.

They descended the staircase and went into the family room. There was a large stone statue of a manticore standing at attention, next to the fireplace. It looked exactly like one of the larger females, with an unruly mane and a cruel expression on her human face. Another statue of a smaller female manticore was positioned on its back as if warding off an attack, her mouth caught in a permanent stone snarl. The pair dominated the room so much that Molly couldn't believe she didn't see them or run into them the night before. She must have been so terrified that she didn't even see the statues.

"Wow, those almost look real," she observed as she stretched out a hand to touch the closest one. "I don't know how I missed them before but I'm glad I did. They look so realistic—just like the real ones I saw out in the backyard."

"You didn't see them when you came through here earlier because they weren't here," he explained. "These aren't statues of manticores... they *are* the manticores... two of them anyway. They've been turned to stone." He pointed towards the kitchen. "There are two more in there, by the back door. Something was here with you. Something that could turn an entire pack of manticores into stone without becoming poisoned hamburger in the process."

She clutched his arm. "Do you think it's still around here?" she asked in a fearful voice.

"I don't know. If it is, I don't think it means us harm. Not just yet anyway. Otherwise I wouldn't have gotten to you." He eyed the statues. "How many manticores did you see last night?"

She thought about it for a few moments. "Eight, maybe nine I think," she responded. "There was Primus, three females and some cubs. The cubs were rolling around and it was getting kind of dark so I'm not sure if there were four or five of them."

"Well there are five stone cubs out back by the pool under a tree," he replied with a certain stiffness to his voice.

She felt a small pang of sadness as she remembered the cubs happily playing and lapsed into silence.

"By the way, did you ever retrieve what you were sent here to find in the first place?" he asked, changing the subject.

"Yeah. I have it right here." She handed him the box, still wrapped in torn curtains. He carefully unwrapped it and shook it, but it sounded empty. "Still..." he mumbled to himself, "I wonder..." He turned it over three times and opened it. When he saw what it contained, his features contorted into a mask of rage.

"That little..." he exclaimed, "...risking your life for this!" He slammed the lid closed. "Come on, let's go. We have to return the Leprechaun's treasure to him." He handed the box back to her. "Here, hang on to this."

Even though he was hobbling on crutches, she still had a hard time keeping up with him as he stormed through the house. As they passed through the family room and into the kitchen, she caught sight of the Primus posed with one great claw lifted and a snarl frozen on his stone face as if he was about to attack. His tail was lifted over his head and the needles were pointed at a spot a few feet in front of him. She lingered for a moment, mesmerized.

Mr. Cotton put a reassuring hand on her shoulder. "There's not much that can stare down a full grown manticore like that," he remarked as he stared at the frozen beast. "We should hurry up and get out of here in case it's still somewhere close by. I'm not sure if you have an ally or an enemy here." He sounded a little nervous. "However, we shouldn't leave them like this," he said softly.

He stepped over to the large bay window. "Here," he called, "pull that curtain down, okay?" She grabbed it and it tore away. Moonlight flooded the room and fell on the stone beast. With a loud crack and a soft sigh, it slowly crumbled into dust.

"What happened?"

"Being turned to stone is a nasty way to go, even for a manticore," the old man replied with an unusually compassionate tone. "The light from a full moon releases their souls. That's why you don't often see stone creatures." There was another crack and a sigh as the second statue disintegrated.

"So what if there hadn't been a full moon?" She was starting to feel a little bad for the creatures, who only hours ago were trying to hunt her down.

"Oh, they'd only be trapped until dawn. Sunlight works too. In fact it's a little more reliable, since it's stronger and doesn't go through phases."

"What about the others?" she asked as they turned and made their way out the front door.

"The moonlight will reach them before the night is over."

"Sounds like you've seen a lot of this."

"Not really. From time to time I've run across an unlucky cat or dog who crossed paths with the basilisk. But I've never seen anything like this before. Stoney-gazers are usually shy, reclusive creatures who only fight back when they feel threatened. This was definitely an attack. To wipe out a complete pride—even cubs…" He shook his head in disbelief.

She snapped her fingers as she remembered something. "Oh my goodness!"

He turned to her. "What is it?"

"Earlier—when I was on my way to see the Leprechaun— something spoke to me from that big bush by the park. It said something about a 'stony gazer…'" she trailed off, trying to recollect the conversation. "Oh, I remember now! It said I was being followed by one."

He frowned. "Did it tell you anything else?"

"No, not really. It was sneezing something terrible."

"This isn't good. It's probably still close by." He paused at the front door and looked around. When he was certain there was nothing waiting to ambush them, he took her hand. "Let's go. Marcus is waiting."

CHAPTER 22

M r. Cotton pulled a small whistle from his shirt pocket and put it to his lips. Molly didn't hear anything and supposed it was like a dog whistle—silent to human ears. There was a whinny and a shadow passed overhead. She looked up to see the familiar winged horse silhouetted against the moon. He gleamed in the moonlight as if made of silver. Circling them once, he landed close by. "Come on," he nickered and tossed his head. "You're not safe."

"Did you see what did this?" Mr. Cotton asked as he climbed onto Marcus's back. "Something turned the entire pride to stone." He extended a hand and pulled Molly up in front of him.

"No, all I could see was the bushes rustling on the far side of the yard. But I smell danger," the horse replied. "And I saw the cubs. Bad business to kill off young, but I suppose leaving a litter of orphaned manticores is worse." He turned and nuzzled Molly's leg. "Hello, Molly. I'm glad we found you. Are you set?"

She nodded and patted the top of his head. "I'm glad you found me too. Thank you!" She settled herself and grabbed his mane with both hands. "I guess I'm as ready as I'll ever be."

"Hang on!" With that he took a few steps and leapt into the air.

Molly looked down in wonder as the sprawling development opened up below them. With its circular streets doubling back on one another, it really did resemble a labyrinth. The house they had just left was on the ridge of a small hill that rose in the center. She spotted the road that she had taken—it snaked though the center of the complex in an almost direct path to the manticore's home.

Marcus banked hard to the left and she clung tighter to his neck to keep from toppling off. The wind whipped around her and cut through her light sweatshirt, chilling her to the bone. Mr. Cotton said something to her, but his words were lost on the wind. The horse turned towards the east and began to descend.

A few minutes later they landed on the sidewalk outside of the convenience store where Cornelius lived. Everything was dark—it was well past closing time and the ancient storekeeper was no doubt home in bed. She looked at her watch but it had stopped at 5:30 and she knew it was past that. Now that she was safely away from danger, realization hit her. "Oh jees! It's gotta be late. Mom's gonna kill me!"

"Relax," Mr. Cotton replied. "I told your mom that I asked you to go pick up some medicine for me and that you got detained by the pharmacy. I apologized and said we had no idea it would take that long and that I'd go pick you up so you wouldn't have to walk home in the dark. She seemed pretty relieved and even called you a good kid for being so helpful."

"I guess that's not too far from the truth… wonder what she'd think if she knew you picked me up and flew me back on a winged horse!"

"Well, sometimes it's better not to tell the entire story. No need to worry your mother unnecessarily," he grumbled, wagging a finger in front of her face.

He dismounted and helped Molly down. "Thank you, my dear friend," he addressed Marcus. "We're forever in your debt."

The flying horse extended a leg and gave an equine version of a bow. "My pleasure. It's the least I can do for those who did so much for me." He tossed his head. "Shall I wait?"

"It's not necessary. Besides, I left my car here when I met you earlier."

Marcus whinnied with laughter. "Right. I'd forgotten." He lifted his wings. "Well then, goodbye, Barnaby Cotton. Goodbye Molly…"

"Wait!" She cried and grabbed his neck in a bear hug. "I miss you."

"I miss you as well. But I know we'll see each other in happier times," Marcus nickered. "Until then, keep the hair I gave you close. I'll come if you need me again."

"Okay." She stepped away and drew the vial from her pocket and lifted it up to show him. "I'll keep it with me always."

He flapped his wings and lifted into the sky. He circled twice overhead and then flew towards the south. She watched him until he was nothing more than a small speck silhouetted against the moon. Then he disappeared completely.

"Well, now it's down to business," Mr. Cotton grumbled. "I have a bone to pick with that no-good, rotten scoundrel…" He hobbled over to the door to the shop and took something out of his pocket that resembled an old fashioned key. "Skeleton key," he explained as he fitted it into the keyhole. "Works on just about anything." There was a click as the door unlocked. He threw it open and stormed down the aisle towards the vending machine. Molly had to jog to keep up with him, despite the fact that he was on crutches.

"Cornelius!" he bellowed. "Come out and show yourself!"

There was a rustle and a squeak and suddenly a tiny mouse darted out from behind the soda machine. Mr. Cotton deftly blocked its way with one of his shoes. "Nice try," he addressed the mouse. "Now, get up."

The mouse lengthened and grew until it reached Leprechaun size and shape. Cornelius crouched at the old man's foot, looking embarrassed and guilty.

Barnaby picked up the tiny man by the scruff of his neck. "Care to explain yourself?"

The Leprechaun cringed. "Well I couldn't very well pledge t' help a human—particularly a wee lass—on a suicide mission, without makin' sure she's worthy of me allegiance," he offered up as an explanation.

"So you sent her out on your own suicide mission—to retrieve your treasure. Gold guarded by Primus, one of the cruelest and most deadly manticores ever conceived! You yourself told me once that he was the one creature in the Nine Realms that you were afraid of." He shook the Leprechaun violently. "You thought that was a suitable test for a child?"

"Well, I figured if she could get past Primus and his kin, she'd have a right good chance against them's who stole yer Griffin," Cornelius yawned. "Besides, we both know t' Sphinx pr'bly let her off easy. So me test might a been a wee bit harder t' make up for his leniency."

"You coward!" Mr. Cotton hissed. "I should keep your gold for all the trouble you've caused. She could have... Probably... would have been eaten."

"But she wasn't," the Leprechaun shot back, defensively. "Not a scratch on her bonny head." He shook himself free from Barnaby's grip. "As for me gold," he quipped, "the deal's between me and the wee lass. She promised t' retrieve it, and retrieved it she has." He looked expectantly at Molly, who still held the small box in her hands.

"There's no deal!" Mr. Cotton exclaimed. "You didn't tell her what she was getting into!" He took her arm. "Come on, Molly, and bring the gold. We're finished here."

Molly looked confused. She looked down at the box in her hands. "I don't think I want to keep it. If that's okay. It belongs to him. I think I want to give it back." She held it out it to the Cornelius, who snatched it greedily from her fingers.

Barnaby threw up his hands in disgust.

The Leprechaun opened the lid, his face reflecting the golden light from the glowing contents inside. He was silent for a long time. Finally he looked up at her. "Thank you," he croaked. There were tears in his blue eyes and she thought it looked like something inside him was melting. He reached inside and withdrew a shining doubloon, which he handed to her. "We Leprechauns do not part with gold lightly, lass. Take this coin as a token o' me allegiance—and with it me heartfelt thanks," he said with genuine emotion. "You're not only brave, but yer heart is as pure as newly minted platinum."

Molly took the coin and held it in her hand. It was warm and vibrated slightly, as if it were alive. A faint glow radiated from it. "It's different from the coin Mr. Cotton gave me."

"Aye, Lass. What you see is the magic of true Irish luck infused in t' gold. Tis what makes it so special and prized. But what most don't know is that t' charm won't work when it's stolen."

Mr. Cotton interjected. "I didn't steal that coin, Cornelius."

"That might be, but you might as well have. 'Twas never yours to keep," the Leprechaun growled. "Me gold knows its rightful owner."

The old man opened his mouth to respond, then shut it. He crossed his arms and turned away, but not before Molly caught a glimpse of shame coloring his face.

Cornelius took her hand in his and closed her fingers around the gold piece. "Now, keep that safe," he whispered. "You are but one o' a handful o' humans ever gifted freely with Leprechaun gold and it is a precious gift indeed. Keep that coin next t' your heart and it will come t' your aid when ye need it most." He saluted her dramatically and then disappeared with a pop.

Barnaby scowled at the place where the Leprechaun vanished. "Serves me right," he muttered. "Never should have trusted him."

"It seems like everything turned out okay, Mr. Cotton," she observed as she put the coin into her pocket. "Cornelius got his gold back, I passed his test and the world is rid of a pack of man-eating monsters."

"Yeah," he replied stiffly. "Still, there are some unanswered questions. For example, who turned Primus and his family into stone?"

She yawned. "I don't know, Mr. Cotton. All I know is that I'm really tired and I'm probably going to still have a lot of explaining to do."

He started towards the door. "Come on, child. Let's get you home."

CHAPTER 23

The pair had rounded the corner and were just starting to cross the parking lot when something made them stop in their tracks. A sleek convertible was parked next to Mr. Cotton's battered truck. Miss Gordon was clearly visible in the driver's seat, leafing through a celebrity gossip magazine. It didn't seem like the kind of thing that would captivate her attention. Molly grabbed Mr. Cotton's hand and squeezed it to get his attention. Miss Gordon looked up from her magazine as if she was expecting them.

"Why, Molly Stevens!" She exclaimed a little too enthusiastically. "What a coincidence running into you here!" She got out of the car and strode up to them. Her eyes glittered like frozen pieces of coal and she held out a claw-like hand in greeting. "This must be your neighbor, Merri… I mean, Mr. Cotton, I presume?"

He looked at her outstretched fingers and shoved his own hands deep into his pants pocket. "There's no need for pretenses, Euryale. You know exactly who I am." Molly noticed he averted his eyes and directed his gaze to a spot on the ground.

Molly put her hands in her pocket as well and her fingers touched the Leprechaun gold. She suddenly remembered the manticore and how she kept calm and listened to him rather than running away. That she faced down her fears was what kept her alive. She didn't quite know what Miss Gordon was capable of, but having a conversation with her in a well-lit parking lot couldn't possibly be any worse than facing a pack of manticores alone in a dark, abandoned wasteland. She squared her shoulders, looked the woman straight in the eye and held her breath, waiting for her teacher to say something.

Miss Gordon turned her attention to Mr. Cotton's bandaged leg. "That looks like a nasty injury you have there. Have you sought medical attention for that?"

His jaw hardened and he pulled himself up to his full height. "I've survived worse," he snapped back defiantly.

"Well if you haven't seen a doctor, perhaps you should consult one…" she said with mock sympathy in her voice. "Or perhaps better yet, a priest. I've heard a bite from a sewer alligator can kill a man in seven days."

"Enough, Euryale," he roared. "What do you want?"

She reached into her handbag and pulled out something wrapped in a tissue. "I came to bring you this," she said as she pressed it into his hands. He dropped it as if it were red hot. The wrapping came away, revealing a long claw, painted bright purple and ending in a ragged bloody stump, as if it had been violently torn from its owner. Mr. Cotton's face paled as he knelt to retrieve it. Molly recognized it instantly.

"I figured you might want proof that your Griffin's safely in my care," Miss Gordon hissed. "I dare say this was a little painful for the beast, but nothing compared with what's in store for him should you try and cross me." Her eyes were as cold and blue as frozen steel. She leaned in close to Molly and jabbed a perfectly manicured fingernail into her chest. "As for you, Molly Stevens… I know you've been to see the Sphinx. Are you fool enough to think his trinket will help you defeat me?"

Not waiting for an answer, she turned to Barnaby. "Old man, your days are numbered and soon you will no longer of any concern to me. Until then, if I get any indication that you have any more ideas up your sleeve, involving this girl or any of the Ancients, you'll find your dear pet's head on your doorstep." Somewhere in the distance a bell tolled nine times. "My, my, time has flown. I'm so glad we had this little chat." She turned and returned to her car, high heels pounding like iron hammers on the pavement. "See you in school, Molly." She called out as she revved the engine and sped out of the parking lot.

Molly waited for the last sounds of screeching tires to fade into the distance. Then she turned to Mr. Cotton. "What did she mean about that?"

He avoided meeting her eyes and replied evasively, "About what?"

"About your days being numbered. And what's a sewer alligator? I thought those were urban legends."

He motioned to his leg. "She was talking about this. Sewer alligators aren't alligators at all. They are a type of small water dragon that lives in polluted waterways. They can be harmless or highly venomous, depending on how toxic their environment is." He unwrapped a small area of his bandaged leg. "The one that did this seems to have been swimming in some pretty nasty soup."

"Oh, my goodness! Have you been to the doctor?"

"Not the right kind of doctor." He winced and tried to smile as he rewrapped the bandages. "Let's not dwell on this, okay? I'll be fine."

"If you say so." She didn't really believe him but she knew enough to change the topic. "What on earth was Miss Gordon doing here? That was a little too coincidental."

He nodded. "I'd have to agree," he said quietly. "Especially given what happened tonight. I wonder…"

"You don't think Cornelius is a double agent, do you? He seemed… so… sincere at the end."

"Cornelius? Oh no, he'd be the last person to turn sides. He absolutely despises that… that… monster. She's the one who moved the manticores into that neighborhood so Cornelius couldn't get to his gold. There's no way he would help her. He'd sooner scatter his gold to the five corners of the Nine Realms, roll over and die before doing her bidding." He gathered the claw back into the bloody wrapping. "Perhaps she or one of her minions followed you here earlier and she figured out what you were up to."

"But how would she know we would be here now?"

"That, I'm not sure of. If she knew you were going to face Primus, I don't believe she would expect you to still be alive. Unless…"

"Do you think she was at the house and saved me?"

He frowned. "I don't think so. For one thing, she's not one to sneak around, as I'm sure you noticed. Secondly, Primus was one of her trusted lieutenents—she was perfectly comfortable around him and wouldn't have much reason to kill him, let alone the entire pride."

Molly's eyes got very big. "Is she really that powerful?"

He looked at her with a grim expression. "Euryale is quite a bit more deadly than a family of manticores."

"But Cornelius said she isn't a witch."

"He's right. She's far more dangerous than a witch. Her kind of magic is ancient and terrible—distilled from thousands of years of anger and hatred. There's very few who can withstand her—certainly not Primus."

"Then how…"

"I don't know," he replied in a worried voice. "Whatever the case, I'm certain she knows Primus and his family have been destroyed." He looked down at the claw in his hands, "This is a message. The stakes have just been raised. Clarence will be in mortal danger if we don't get to him soon."

CHAPTER 24

The next afternoon, Molly left Barnaby's house shaking her head. He had just finished giving her directions to find a Mermaid in the middle of the largest shopping mall in Santa Geronimo. She wondered if perhaps Mr. Cotton was getting a little crazy from the fever, but on the other hand, she was getting used to running into magic creatures in the most improbable of places. After all, the Sphinx lived in Union Station. Why couldn't a Mermaid live in a mall?

As she stepped out on the porch she heard the unmistakable sound of cellophane crackling under her foot. She looked down and saw a Slim Jim wrapper on the doormat. *Odd*, she thought. She was pretty sure it wasn't there when she came in only a few minutes before. Picking it up, she held it gingerly between her forefinger and thumb. There were teeth marks in the plastic and bits of Slim Jim still stuck to gobs of saliva. She made a face and tossed the wrapper into a nearby trashcan as she headed towards the bus stop.

The bus dropped her off twenty minutes later in front of the mall. Built to look like an Italian palace, it had two floors of storefronts surrounding a large outdoor courtyard paved in yellow tile. Cascades of pink and white geraniums hung in baskets from beams made to look like carved oak. Molly soon located the three-tiered yellow marble fountain in the center of courtyard. The first and second tiers were shallow bowls of cascading water containing a fair amount of silver and copper coins. The third was a larger basin full of water lilies. Pale pink and white flowers rose on stems that just cleared the surface, giving the appearance that each flower floated on top, surrounded by wide green pads. She easily made out the dull gleam of coins on the bottom and thought the deepest part couldn't be more than a couple of feet. There was no way anything as large as a Mermaid could live in this fountain.

She shrugged and pulled out the small silver whistle Mr. Cotton had given her to call the Mermaid. It was shaped like a bullfrog with the mouth open just enough to form the mouthpiece. She wondered if it had anything to do with the story of the princess kissing a frog. These days she believed anything was possible. Putting her lips to the mouth of the metallic amphibian, she blew gently. It sounded a single clear note like the song of crystal underwater. There was a rustle among the lilies and a small splash. Two frog-like eyes peeped up from underneath a large green lily pad and looked inquisitively at her for a minute. Then the lily pad lifted and the Mermaid's head rose out of the water.

Molly by now was used to the inaccuracy of story books, so she was not at all surprised to see that the Mermaid was not a beautiful girl, a clamshell bikini top and a fish tail. Even so, the creature's appearance was still something of a shock. She had stringy green hair that resembled the long strands of algae often found in standing pools of water. Her eyes were the color of the mud found at the bottom of a well and her lips were so thin they were almost non-existent. When she smiled she exposed two rows of tiny sharp teeth like a piranha's. A slimy hand crawled over the rim of the fountain and hung there, tipped with long webbed fingers.

"Why have you called Rymira, land-dweller?" the Mermaid croaked with a voice that could only come from a being not accustomed to breathing air. "You are not the Green Man."

Molly looked at her for a moment in bewilderment before realization hit. "You mean Mr. Cotton? No, I'm not the Green Man." She held up the whistle. "But he gave me this to call you."

The creature cocked her head in curiosity and repeated her question. "Why do you summon Rymira?"

"I'm sorry to disturb you…" Molly apologized rather formally. "…But I was wondering if you could help me?" By now she knew well that manners were important to making friends, especially when it came to asking favors of magical creatures.

"You said you were sent by the Green Man," the Mermaid observed suspiciously. "What does he ask of Rymira?" She lowered herself back into the water until only her eyes were visible above the surface.

"The Green Man needs your help," Molly replied, unconsciously mimicking the Mermaid's formal way of speaking. "He's terribly hurt and Euryale has kidnapped Clarence."

Rymira looked puzzled for a moment and blinked her wide fishy eyes several times. Then she raised herself back out of the water and peered closely at Molly. "The Green Man knows I cannot interfere in the affairs of lower creatures." She was quiet for a moment. "But, I may have something that might help you on your quest."

"Oh, thank you!" Molly gushed. "I need all the help I can get."

"Not so fast. First, you must be tested to see if you are worthy."

"You guys always seem to want to do that," Molly muttered. "I'm okay if you just give me whatever magic talisman…"

The Mermaid gave her a withering look.

Molly sighed. "Okay, okay, I get it. Test first. Reward afterwards." She squared her shoulders. "Let's get on with it."

"So you think you are ready?" Rymira laughed, which sounded like waves breaking on the coast. "Come closer, Land-Dweller."

Molly stepped up to the fountain and suddenly a pair of strong arms grabbed her and pulled her into the water. She extended her hands to protect her head from slamming into the bottom of the shallow pond, but was surprised to find that once she went below the surface, it was much deeper than she expected. She realized now that a powerful enchantment hid the true nature of the pool from unwanted visitors. The Mermaid dragged her deeper and deeper into the dark until Molly wasn't able to see her hands in front of her eyes. Long trails of algae wrapped themselves around her and entangled her arms and legs like green cobwebs. She shut her eyes and held her breath. Just when she thought her lungs would burst, she was suddenly pulled out of the water again and lying on a hard cold surface. She wiped away a strand of algae that was caught across her face and opened her eyes again.

To her amazement, she found herself in a grotto on the edge of a vast underwater lake. There was an eerie glow that she realized came from moss growing on the walls. It bathed the cave in a greenish light that made everything look slimy. The air was heavy and thick and smelled strongly like the bottom of a pond. Molly crinkled her nose up and looked around. The Mermaid was a little ways away, propped up on bony elbows and staring up at her with big lamp-like eyes.

Rymira was much larger than she appeared to be in the fountain—almost as tall as Molly if she stood straight up on her tail. Her skin was not scaly, but resembled that of a frog or salamander—sort of a translucent olive color with dark green spots. Her torso ended in a tail with tiny wizened legs on either side, much like a tadpole who is beginning to turn into a frog. Her stringy hair turned out not to be hair at all but rather a tangle of algae fastened to her head like a human might wear a wig or a hairpiece. An ornate comb inlaid with mother-of pearl held it in place. Her nose was flat with small nostrils set high on the bridge and her mouth was too wide for her face. There is nothing really fish-like about her at all, Molly observed.

"Is this what you really look like? Or is it more…"

"…Glamour? No, this is my real appearance," Rymira croaked. "I have no reason to hide from a friend of the Green Man. Do I look strange to you?"

Molly wasn't sure what to say. The Mermaid was one of the strangest looking creatures she'd encountered so far, but she knew better than to voice that opinion. She looked at her feet.

The Mermaid watched Molly expectantly for a moment before finally changing the subject. "I have brought you here, because this is where your test begins." She lifted one thin bony arm off the ground, grabbed an algae-covered outcropping of rock and pulled herself up until she was at eye level. Molly marveled at how strong those thin arms were as she remembered how effortlessly they pulled her into the water. Rymira pointed a long webbed finger at the far end of the cave, directly behind where Molly crouched. "Over there is a mirror. You must look into it," she gasped.

Molly squinted her eyes and looked backwards, but the mirror was obscured. "Then what?"

Rymira shrugged.

"That's it?" Molly cried with astonishment. "You mean that's all I have to do?"

The Mermaid laughed. "Is that all you have to do? Yes, Land-Dweller, that is all you have to do. It will be enough." With that, she executed an elaborate backwards flip into the water and disappeared.

Molly sat there alone and stunned for several minutes, green water dripping from the ceiling and staining her T-shirt. Looking into a mirror seemed so simple, but she suspected from the Mermaid's sarcastic tone that there was something more to the test than that. But without Rymira's help, there was no way to escape the grotto and Molly was pretty sure she wouldn't be allowed to leave until she had looked into the mirror.

She waited, hoping the Mermaid would come back to explain things a little more clearly. But several minutes went by without even a ripple in the water. After she was sure the Mermaid wasn't going to resurface any time soon, Molly got up and started to walk towards the back of the cave.

She had barely taken more than a few steps when a loud splash behind her made her jump. She whirled around just in time to see Rymira pulling herself up on the stone outcropping again. "I see you have not yet gone to the mirror," the Mermaid said rather disdainfully. "I suppose you are waiting to know more… like what waits inside it."

"Well," Molly replied, trembling, "I was a little worried. You see, there was this Leprechaun and he told me…"

"I know what the Leprechaun did, Land-Dweller," the Mermaid interrupted curtly. "I am not so misdirected as he. I have no reason to send you into unwarranted danger. The Green Man knows this."

"I'm sorry. I didn't mean to suggest that you were like him. I'm just a little nervous after last time, that's all."

"Of course, land-dweller." She relaxed, accepting Molly's apology with a wave of one arm. "You are wise to be cautious. The mirror will show you things you may not want to see."

"Oh, is it a magic mirror that will show me the future?" Molly was pretty sure she could manage to pass that kind of test.

"No, silly human," the Mermaid croaked. "This mirror has much more powerful magic. It will show you who you really are."

Molly grinned. "Piece of cake." There were a zillion stories about those kinds of mirrors. The hero always went before the mirror and had to battle his own worst demons. She didn't have any demons. She was just a boring little girl with a boring life up until a few weeks ago. The mirror wouldn't show her anything she couldn't handle.

The Mermaid stared at her with big unblinking eyes. "Suit yourself." She slid off the rock into the pool and was gone.

CHAPTER 25

Molly shivered in her wet clothes, alone once more. She turned and headed towards the back of the cave. As she crept closer, she thought she saw an opening cut into the far end, partially hidden behind a large boulder. The farther she moved away from the magic pool, the dimmer the illuminating moss became. Once she went inside the tunnel, the last vestiges of light disappeared completely, cloaking her in blackness. She felt her way blindly along a dark corridor until she rounded a bend and found herself in a low-ceilinged room. It was illuminated with a soft white glow that didn't seem to originate from any particular source.

Something oval-shaped hung on the wall, covered by a black cloth. She touched it and felt the soft plush of velvet crush against a hard smooth surface under her fingertips. She carefully grabbed a corner and lifted it just enough to expose part of a carved frame, covered in gold leaf and set with pearls and sea-shells. She knew immediately that this must be the mirror Rymira spoke of. With a loud exhale, she pulled the cloth away and let it fall to the floor.

Instead of seeing herself reflected back at her, she saw nothing. The mirror was completely black. *A magic mirror... she thought as her courage returned. This isn't really a test at all, compared to the Sphinx and his blood-sucking roses and getting past that pack of manticores.* She stepped confidently up to the mirror and peered into the darkened glass—it looked singed. She wondered what could have caused the silver backing of a mirror to turn black like that. "Poor mirror. Looks like someone set you on fire and burnt the magic right out of you."

She waited.

Nothing happened.

She sighed, wondering if she was missing something. *Maybe I'm supposed to recite a spell...* She racked her brain for something appropriate, but only one thing came to mind.

"Mirror, mirror, on the wall, who's the fairest one of all?"

The mirror remained black.

"Oh, for Pete's sake!" She stamped impatiently. "Why do magic things alway have to have some catch?" She turned to go but something inside her told her to stay a few minutes longer. *Just wait.* She looked deeper, almost touching her nose to the glass. Suddenly there was movement within the mirror. A thick fog quickly filled it, swirling ominously under the glass. Within a few seconds the black was completely obscured by the pale mist.

A deep voice boomed from the mirror. "You will be shown two possible futures. Either may come to pass. Choose wisely."

The mist cleared. She watched as a scene unfolded and began to play itself out.

Thunder cracked the sky with a deafening rumble. Molly stood on her porch looking across the street where a familiar figure beckoned. Miss Gordon, dressed in a white raincoat and surrounded by strange creatures that wove around her as if made of smoke, raised her hand again. "Molly," she called out. "I'd like to have a word with you."

Molly stepped off her porch and crossed the street. "I'm not afraid of you," she lied.

Miss Gordon gave her a queer smile. "You should be. I don't think you understand what you've gotten yourself into. Or what could happen... to you... your mother... your little brother..." Her eyes glittered like ice.

On the other side of the mirror, Molly shuddered. *My family… It never occured to her that anyone but Clarence and Mr. Cotton could be in danger.*

Miss Gordon knelt until she was eye to eye with Molly. "This is old business between Jonas and I and he never should have brought you into it. I'm so sorry you got caught up in this feud." In an almost maternal fashion, she pulled Molly's hood up over her head against the rain that was now beginning to come down. "Now, I don't have any reason to hurt you, so perhaps we can come to an agreement before anything else happens."

"Like what?" Molly asked suspiciously.

"Well, I believe there's a sewer alligator still loose in this neighborhood," Miss Gordon replied in a soothing voice. "How would you like me to make it go away?" She stood up. "In fact, what if I made sure you and your family were always safe from danger? You'd never have to worry about trolls, dragons… manticores…" Her voice lingered on the last word, drawing it out dramatically.

"What would I have to do?"

"Just walk back into your house and stay there until the storm is over. Already your magic Sight is starting to fade and when it does you can't revive it without the lilies. Even if you wanted to, you couldn't save the Griffin without the magic. It would be such a waste to see you die. You really are a brave girl."

"So what happens if I go back inside?"

"When you wake up tomorrow, you can be a normal little girl with a normal life again. No more looking over your shoulder to see if you're being followed… or hunted. It will be like none of this ever happened and the last few weeks were nothing but a bad dream. Wouldn't you like that?"

Molly nodded. "But what about Mr. Cotton… and Clarence?"

"It's too late for Jonas, I'm afraid. Already he's drawing his last breath, and once he does then our feud will be thankfully over. There's nothing you— or anyone else—can do to save him. As for Clarence and the others, I have no grudge with them—they'll be set free into the Nine Realms. They'll be safe… and so will you and your family. You have my word." She extended her hand. "Do we have a deal?"

Molly paused for a moment. "I guess so. I don't want to die and I don't want anything to happen to my mom and Dylan." She clasped Miss Gordon's hand and shook it. There was a flash and everything vibrated for a split second, as if a tiny earthquake had hit the ground right under their feet. "What was that?"

"The deal is bound with magic," Miss Gordon said. "Neither of us can go back on our word."

The mist swirled and closed around them. When it lifted, the mirror showed Molly her own bedroom. It was the next morning, she supposed, from the bright light streaming in her window.

Molly dressed and went downstairs. Opening the door, she looked outside. Everything was bright, washed clean by the heavy rain the night before. She looked next door. The small tidy bungalow had a real estate sign posted in front. She tried to remember who lived there but it seemed like the house had been vacant forever. She shook her head and went back inside to watch TV.

The mirror darkened and everything went black. Molly looked around. "I don't need to see the second choice! There's no way I'd ever make a deal with Miss Gordon!"

The deep voice filled the cavern and echoed off the walls. "You will be shown two possible futures. Either may come to pass. Choose wisely."

"But I'm telling you—I don't need to see anything more. I'm not going to betray my friends!"

The mirror began to fill with smoke again. When it cleared the conversation between Molly and Miss Gordon played exactly as before.

Miss Gordon extended her hand. "Do we have a deal?"

Molly shoved her hands in her pockets and backed away. "No. I can't betray my friends. I don't care what happens."

Miss Gordon shook her head. "As you wish." She turned and walked away, her minions trailing behind her like greasy black smoke. There was a flash of lightning so bright that Molly shut her eyes. When she opened them, Miss Gordon was gone.

Mist obscured the scene. It faded to show Molly the inside of her kitchen.

The microwave chimed and Molly removed a steaming cup of hot cocoa. She went into the living room and stared at the thunderheads. Suddenly there was a crash and a wail from the direction of her room. As soon as her mind registered that it was coming from her brother, the cry was cut off in midstream.

Dylan!

She raced upstairs. Her room was in shambles. Dylan lay on his bed, unmoving and silent. "Dylan," she whispered. "Hey, did you have a bad dream? He was pale and cold. She held her hand up to his face. There was only the slightest movement of air between his lips. "Dylan! Wake up!" She picked him up but he lay limp in her arms. "Mom!" She cried and set him back down on his bed. "Mom!" She ran into the hall but her mother's door was still shut. She flung the door open. "Mom! Why don't you answer..."

Her mother lay silent on her bed as well. Even from across the room Molly could see that she was barely breathing. "No!"

She ran back into her bedroom and noticed for the first time that her jewelry box was smashed on the floor. Everything was scattered... except...

The talismans that would help her defeat Miss Gordon were gone.

Mist closed around the scene in the mirror. Molly felt an icy lump starting to form in the pit of her stomach. For the first time she began to question her loyalty to her friends. *What have I done?*

She asked herself. The mist swirled within the mirror for a long time before revealing another scene.

Miss Gordon faced her, and this time she had completely dropped her magic disguise. Molly barely recognized her. Although the creature in front of her had Miss Gordon's patrician face, her skin was covered in lumpy tumorous scales and she had a snakelike mouth, complete with fangs and a forked tongue. Her hair was a mane of wriggling snakes and her torso ended in a reptilian tail. She balanced herself upright, like a cobra. "You made a fatal mistake, Molly Stevens. Now you and everyone close to you will pay the price. As soon as I am finished with you, I'll make good on my promise. The Griffin is as good as dead. Your family is already under my enchantment— their hearts will continue to beat slower and slower until they finally stop." She took a step forward and her eyes glowed. A fly buzzed in front of her face and dropped to the floor. "As for you… you'll make a nice addition to my collection…"

Molly looked at the floor where the fly had fallen. It lay broken in several pieces. "You… you turned it to stone!"

Miss Gordon laughed. "Yes, my dear. And you are next. She lifted her gaze and Molly found she could not look away…

Mercifully, the mist obscured the mirror once more and it slowly darkened again. The scene was over. But it was enough. Molly backed away from the mirror and sat down heavily on the floor.

"You have been shown two possible futures. Either may come to pass. Choose wisely."

This time Molly wasn't quite so quick to respond. "I know," she whispered in a very small voice. "But how can I choose? Either I betray my friends… or my family and I die…" Tears welled up in her eyes. "I'm just a kid!" She cried. "How do I know what's right?"

CHAPTER 26

Molly stepped out of the cleft in the grotto, pale and shaking. She carefully made her way back to the edge of the pool, where Rymira waited. The Mermaid lifted herself high on the outcropping of rock and looked into Molly's tear stained face, as if reading her soul. "I see you faced the challenge of the mirror, Land-Dweller," she observed. "How choose you?"

Molly's voice trembled. "I can't betray Mr. Cotton and Clarence. You have to help me. I don't want my brother and mom to get hurt... but..." she trailed off as she started to cry. "I can't do it. I just can't live with abandoning Clarence and Mr. Cotton... and all the others. I have to try to save him... somehow, I'd rather die myself than run away like a coward."

"Is this the choice you make?" Rymira croaked.

Molly nodded and gulped. "Is it the right one?"

"What does your heart tell you?"

"It's funny, but when I thought about being safe and just going back to who I was... well it didn't feel right. Like I was making a huge mistake."

The Mermaid smiled. "You chose like a true hero. One who has the strength of character to face Euryale and defeat her." She slid off the rock into the water. "You have passed my test." Suddenly she hissed and put her hand up to her lips, signaling for Molly to be quiet. For several moments, there was nothing but the sound of water lapping against the rocks.

"I don't hear anything except the water," Molly whispered as quietly as she could.

"Exactly," Rymira whispered back. "No frogs… No birds." She dipped one long finger into the pool and remained motionless, as if she might be listening to the ripples in the water. "Be very still. It's out there—seeking you."

Molly froze. She opened her mouth to ask, but a shake of the Mermaid's head silenced her. They stayed silent for what seemed like an eternity. Then when Molly thought she couldn't stand it any longer, the croak of a bullfrog broke the silence.

"I think it's left my pool," Rymira whispered. "But let me be sure." She slid quietly into the water and disappeared.

Molly sat down and drew her legs in tightly against the cold dampness. She tucked her head into her chin and closed her eyes. The lump in her stomach had grown into a cold hard rock. Had she really just condemned her family to certain death?

A splash startled her and she looked up to see the Mermaid pulling herself back up on shore by one lanky arm. "We're safe for now. It has gone away," she announced without any more explanation of what 'it' was or why it had left. "But we must hurry. Time grows short for the Green Man." She rolled a large stone away from the cave wall to reveal a small cavity behind it. Reaching a long webbed finger into the space, she removed a shiny object from its hiding place and held it out to Molly.

Molly took it and turned the object over in her hands. It was a small silver case that looked like the type made to hold cigarettes. Her grandfather used to have one just like it. However when she opened this one, she discovered that it wasn't like his at all. Both sides folded open into two flat pieces and then fit together into one big piece. One side was highly polished silver that reflected like a mirror. However, there was no glass to be broken and thus doom its owner to seven years of bad luck. "Lucky mirror," she remarked. "No chance of you breaking." She looked over at the Mermaid. "Miss Gordon's a stony gazer—will she turn to stone if she sees her reflection? Like Medusa?"

"Euryale is much more dangerous. But nevertheless, the mirror will serve you well," Rymira replied. "Take it with some advice... If you are one who listens..."

"Yes, of course I'll listen. Please, I can use all the help I can get."

"You have undergone three challenges. What have you learned?"

"Huh?" Molly was puzzled.

The Mermaid tried again. "What is the most important thing you are taking from here?"

Molly pondered this for a minute and almost answered, "the mirror." But there was something odd about the way Rymira asked, which made it sound suspiciously like a trick question. She recollected everything that happened after she met the Mermaid. After a moment she replied excitedly, "The most important thing isn't the mirror you gave me, but what I learned, isn't it? It's that I should listen to my heart when I have to make a tough choice."

"Very good," the Mermaid nodded her head in approval.

"So the reward for passing each test isn't really the Sphinx's pendant, the Leprechaun's coin or your mirror," Molly mused.

"Exactly," the Mermaid agreed, "Although they are each powerful tools in their own right, and will help and protect you when you face your enemy, the real treasure is the wisdom you gained from each task you were given. "

Molly thought long and hard. "From the Sphinx I learned to follow instructions... and that sometimes it's not good to overfeed the flowers," she chuckled.

"...And not to fear the unknown," Rymira added.

Molly grinned and continued. "Yeah. From the Leprechaun I learned to be calm and to use my head..." she snapped her fingers. "Oh yeah! Sometimes it's better to keep my mouth shut and listen."

"That's a very important lesson indeed. Few humans ever understand the power of listening."

"Finally, your magic mirror taught me to listen to my heart. But it also showed me how to defeat Miss Gordon." She paused and looked at her feet. "But I don't think I would have seen how to do that if it weren't for the Sphinx. He said the smallest details are sometimes the most important."

Rymira nodded. "He is very wise. You were smart to remember and heed his advice, land-dweller. Are you ready to return to your world?"

Molly put the silver mirror safely away in her pocket and extended her hand. The Mermaid took it and together they entered the pool. Molly shut her eyes once more and felt strands of algae slip across her face as she was pulled through the cool water. She felt her face break the surface of the fountain and almost immediately experienced a very strange sensation, as if she was being stretched in several directions at once. When she opened her eyes, she found herself back on the stone tiles looking into the fountain. Her clothes and hair were dry and there was no indication she had ever left the spot where she was standing.

She glanced over at the large clock mounted in front of a jewelry store several doors away—it read 3:38. *That can't be right*, she thought. She checked her watch to confirm and frowned. *How can this be?* According to the clock and her watch, she was underwater in the Mermaid's grotto for less than two minutes. She wondered for a moment if it had all been a dream, until she slid her hand into her pocket and felt the boxy shape of the silver mirrorcase.

There was a small splash and Molly looked up to see Rymira peering out at her from under a lily pad. She was much smaller now—hardly much bigger than a large bullfrog. "You better get back. The Green Man is waiting for you."

"Thanks!" Molly waved and turned to go.

"Wait," Rymira called. "There's one last thing you should know." Her voice was little more than a whisper.

Molly leaned in close.

"When things seem darkest, help will come from an unexpected source. Keep your eyes sharp and your mind open."

CHAPTER 27

Early the next morning, Molly woke to the sound of Dylan softly snoring in his bed. She opened her eyes and groaned, realizing it was not yet light. She lay in bed for a long time, trying to will herself back to sleep, without success. When she finally gave up and decided to get out of bed, the sky was just starting to glow pink on the eastern horizon.

A large brown moth buzzed against her window as it tried to escape. She recognized it as a sphinx moth and thought about her encounter with its namesake. "Look at you," she addressed it in a whisper. "You really don't look anything like a sphinx at all." It buzzed harder at the sound of her voice and bumped against the windowpane, desperately trying to find a way out. She watched the insect for a few moments; it was too frantic right now for her to safely remove it without causing injury. As it turned away from the window and tried a different approach, Molly saw a flash of the moth's pink under-wings. They matched the colors of the sunrise outside.

She padded downstairs to the living room and curled up on the sofa, watching the dawn from the front window. Ominous looking dark clouds gathered in a crimson sky. She was reminded of a funny poem about the weather that her nana used to recite all the time: Red sky at night, sailors' delight. *Red sky in the morning, sailors' warning.* Molly didn't need an old superstitious saying about the weather to know that a storm was brewing. The big black thunderheads were enough.

She went into the kitchen and made herself a cup of hot chocolate in the microwave. She had a bad feeling about this day. It felt like the period of waiting before a math test that she hadn't studied for, except worse. As she took a sip of the comforting warm drink, she thought about everything she had been through. It seemed like so long ago that she tried to pick the black lily in her yard. She smiled as she thought about how silly she was to think she was being poisoned. *So childish.*

Suddenly the silence was broken by a crash and a howl from upstairs. It was Dylan, no doubt falling out of bed again. She had the strangest feeling of *déjà vu* until she remembered the vision from the mirror. *Oh… no!* She dashed upstairs, just as Dylan's cry was cut off.

Don't let this be happening… not like this, she thought as she shut her eyes and opened the door. True to the vision the magic mirror had shown her, the room was in shambles—her closet mirror shattered into pieces. Dylan lay pale and still on his bed. "No! She cried. "It's not fair! I never talked to Miss Gordon. I didn't make any choices."

But you did, she reminded herself. *You told the Mermaid that you'd choose your friends…*

"But…. But… I didn't think this would really happen…" She rushed over and tried to wake her little brother, but it was no use. She started to cry as she only now began to understand the severity of her decision. "I'm so sorry, Dylan. I never meant for you to get hurt."

A sick realization hit her. *If the mirror was showing me the truth, then…* She glanced over to her dresser and paled. Someone had gone through her jewelry box where her talismans were kept. The small wooden box was upturned and the contents strewn all over the floor—ticket stubs, shells picked up from her favorite Maui beaches, a silver ring, three pairs of mismatched earrings and a pin from an airline. But the amber pendant given to her by the Sphinx and the coin from the Leprechaun were both gone. Trying to stay calm, she searched through the clothes littering the floor until she located the pants she wore yesterday. She felt around for the front pocket and relaxed a little as her fingers closed around the Mermaid's tiny mirror case. It was a lucky thing that she had forgotten to put it away with her other treasures the night before. Still the loss of the pendant and coin unnerved her.

Suddenly she noticed something that the mirror hadn't shown her—a large familiar black feather lay on her pillow. She recognized it immediately as Clarence's. The shaft was broken and looked as if it had been removed by force. A small stone insect lay next to the feather. She gasped with horror as she recognized it as the sphinx moth. The window was still locked from the inside, but there was a funny dark blotch in the center, as if a ball of soot had exploded against the glass. She touched the spot and a sticky residue came away on her fingers. It smelled acrid, like burning plastic. Glancing outside, a cold shiver crawled up her spine as she recognized the unmistakable figure of Miss Gordon, dressed in the same white raincoat the mirror had shown her wearing the day before. They locked eyes for just a moment before the tall woman turned and walked swiftly down the street in the direction of the park.

CHAPTER 28

Molly threw on her clothes and raced over to Mr. Cotton's house. The black storm clouds were overhead now and the street was empty. The first raindrops spattered her neighbor's ruined lawn, sending up small clouds of dust as they hit the dry earth. One hit her squarely on the bridge of her nose as she rushed up to the porch. She looked around as she pushed the doorbell, fearful of being watched. She didn't hear the usual tolling of the doorbell chimes so she grabbed the knocker. The old man opened the door before she had a chance to use it. He took one look at her tearstained face and puffy eyes and ushered her in quickly. "Wait here," he said as he stepped out onto the porch and shut the door behind him. After a moment he came back inside. There were three loud clicks as he fastened all three deadbolts.

"Euryale's nearby," he spat. "I smell the rancid stink of her minions."

Molly nodded, pale and frightened. "She was in my house." Her voice caught as she choked back sobs. "My mom… Dylan… Miss Gordon put some kind of spell on them and now they won't wake up."

"Are you sure?"

She nodded. "Rymira's magic mirror showed me. But… but…" She broke down crying. "I guess I didn't really think it would happen."

He put a hand across her shoulder. "Shhhhh… Take a deep breath and try to calm down. I need you to tell me the whole story. Asleep you said? They're still breathing?"

"Yeah, but barely. Yesterday the mirror showed me Miss Gordon and she said she enchanted them so their hearts would slow down and stop. But… I… I thought… well, I don't know what I thought. I guess I didn't think it would really happen!"

"Molly, I don't know what you're talking about. Mirrors… Enchantments… Can you start from the beginning?"

She took a deep breath and recounted the story from the moment she stepped off the bus. After she told him about her experience with the magic mirror, he stopped her. "You told me you had seen Rymira and that she gave you another talisman. You didn't say anything about this test. Why not?"

She shifted her weight and looked at her feet. "I knew you would be upset with me if you knew I chose you over my family. You've always told me that family comes first…"

He scowled. "That's very true. Without your family, there really is nothing."

A large tear ran down her cheek and she began to cry again. "You… and Clarence… well… you *are* my family! Just as much as mom and Dylan! Anyway, Rymira said I made the right choice."

"She did?"

"She said I should always listen to my heart… and it told me it was wrong to run away."

Mr. Cotton sat down hard on the sofa with a grimace of pain. "She's correct in most cases. But this is different…"

"Why?"

"Because there's really no point in trying to save me, I'm afraid. I don't have much time left." With some effort, he pulled up the leg of his pants. Black venom formed a spider web pattern all the way up past his knee as it spread through the capillaries just under his skin.

"You're dying! Just like Miss Gordon said!"

He let the pants leg fall and looked away. "Finish your story."

She told him the rest of what happened, choking back sobs when she spoke of how she found her brother and mother unconscious. She ended with the theft of the magic items and finding the feather and stone moth on her pillow. Mr. Cotton's expressions were mixed and hard to read. Sometimes he looked angry but at other times he looked sorrowful. When she was finished he motioned for her to sit beside him. For several minutes there was no sound save the sound of his labored breathing.

Finally he broke the silence. "Were you there when she enchanted your family?"

"I... I was downstairs," she stammered.

"It's apparent she came to rob you of the talismans, not to harm you. Even your mother and brother were spared... in a fashion. She could have done far worse."

She scowled. "Worse?"

"She put a sleeping charm on them. She could have turned them to stone, like she did the moth. But she didn't. That says a lot."

"What do you mean?" she asked hopefully.

"I don't believe Euryale considers you a real threat. She underestimates you, as many grownups tend to do with people your age," he explained. "She must think that it is enough to simply frighten you and take away your protective charms. Otherwise she wouldn't have left without... well... making sure you... and I mean *all* of you... weren't a threat anymore."

Molly shivered. The thought of Dylan and her mother turned to stone was almost too much to bear. "She's won, hasn't she? She took everything!"

"Not everything, child," the old man replied gently. "You said she didn't take the mirror the Mermaid gave you."

"Yeah... I guess she didn't find it."

"Euryale hasn't seen you in school since before you visited the Mermaid. In fact," he added, "I'd be willing to bet she has no idea that you've passed the third trial and therefore doesn't know you've got the last talisman."

"Would she know there was was third trial?"

"Well of course she would," he scoffed. "There's always three tests. Everyone knows that."

She thought about it for a second and realized that he was right. Magic always seemed to come in threes. It didn't occur to her until now that it might be by design. "Is it a rule?"

"Not a written-down-rule," he answered. "It's just the way things are. "Just like there's no rule that says that the sky is above us and the earth is under our feet. It just is."

She nodded her head, beginning to feel hopeful. "So Miss Gordon probably assumes that since there needs to be three tests, I haven't found the third talisman yet..." she trailed off and looked at him. "...And maybe that I'm scared enough by her visit this morning to call the whole thing off."

"Exactly."

"But mom and Dylan. What about them?"

"They're safe, for now anyway. Miss Gordon did tell you the truth about one thing—there is an old feud between she and I." He paused and let out a heavy, tired sigh. "Maybe if I surrender myself to her, she'll let everyone go."

"Do you really believe that?"

"What other choice do I have? Either way I'm a dead man. There's no cure for this."

"You told me once Griffins could heal poison. Clarence could save you, couldn't he?"

He said nothing, but the way he avoided her eyes told her that she was right. "We'll have to think of some other way. You can't do this."

She dug around her pocket. "But I still have the mirror Rymira gave me..." Her voice suddenly trailed off as her fingers wrapped around something in her pocket and pulled it out. "What the?" She slowly opened her hand to reveal a cigarette case, so encrusted by rust that there was no way it could be opened. "What happened? This can't be the mirror..."

Mr. Cotton's face blanched. "Oh dear." He pulled something out of his pocket and held it out to her. "What do you see?"

She squinted. "It looks like a little piece of rolled up leaf."

He slumped back and groaned. "It's finally happened."

Realization hit her like a punch to the stomach. "Oh no, the Sight. It's gone, isn't it? That's not really a leaf... It's that shoe you showed me before."

He nodded sadly. "I'm afraid so. It's over."

"There's got to be another way. I have to get Clarence now. I'll just have to go without magic. I mean I'll still be able to find him. He'll just be a little dog again."

"Molly, this is no game. Even if I were to let you go, you won't be able to get past her guards without the Sight. It's much too dangerous. You're just as blind to magic now as I am." He winced in pain and a gasp escaped his lips. "It's a lost cause."

She jumped up from the couch. "Wait! I've got an idea. The lily on my side of the fence... the one I picked the flower from, what if it's still there?"

He shut his eyes. "No, Molly. It's too late for me. Even if there's another flower on it, I'm too weak to make the trip."

"I could go."

He shook his head. "No, I can't let you do that. We're under strict orders from the constable!"

"But this is your life we're talking about!"

"And yours," he snapped. "I will not have you risking your life! Even if you were able to rescue Clarence in time to save me—which is a long shot by the way—the Magic Compliance Committee has no tolerance for those who break Elven rules. A second offense of unauthorized magic use is punished by death."

"But without Clarence, you'll die," she whined.

He cut her off with a weak wave of his hand. "Not another word. It's over. There's nothing more to be said. Now leave me. I need to get my affairs in order."

Molly ran to the door. "You're wrong! There is another way!" She unlocked the three deadbolts and jerked the door open. "I got you into this mess. I'm going to get you out," she cried as she stepped outside.

The storm was in full force now. Rain pelted the ground, as hard and unforgiving as bullets made of water. She looked around to see if Miss Gordon or her minions were waiting, but the yard and street were empty. Pulling her hoodie over her head against the downpour, she dashed around the corner into her own yard, made for the camellia bush where she last saw the magic flower. She came to the spot where she'd last seen the plant and her breath caught in her throat.

The last vision lily was gone.

CHAPTER 29

Molly dropped to her knees in front of the bush. The lily was gone, ripped up by the roots from the look of the ragged soil. Tears formed in her eyes, only to be washed away by the raindrops. "What do I do now?" she screamed at the sky. Suddenly a flash of lightning revealed a second, smaller lily half concealed behind a clump of ivy. She grabbed the black flower, crushing it into a sticky purple mess in her hand. Taking a deep breath, she stuck purple fingers into both ears and winced as they began to tingle. *I forgot how much this hurts*, she grimaced and looked at her fingers again. The rain was coming down harder now, soaking her and beginning to wash her hands clean. There was no more time—another minute and the last of the juice and her only opportunity to save Mr. Cotton would be gone. She rubbed her fingers into her eyes. As before, her eyes burned and the blindness was immediate. A loud clap of thunder startled her and she scrambled farther under the bush. Cold, wet and frightened, she shivered in blackness. "This will just be a minute… just another minute… please let it be a minute…"

The bush offered no real protection from the torrential downpour. Cold, wet and terrified, she realized that Mr. Cotton was right. *I'm just a kid*, she thought. *There's no way I can save Clarence.*

"Don't be a tellin' yourself such nonsense…" a soft sing-song voice whispered in her ear. "You be a smart girl."

She opened her eyes but her sight was still blurry. "Sphinx?" Her vision cleared and she expected to see the feline, but there was nobody around. "But, I lost the necklace you gave me, as well as the Leprechaun's coin. I can't save Clarence without them."

"Girl, you don't need dem magic charms. You got everytin' you need inside you."

"But Miss Gordon's a stoney-gazer," she moaned. "How can I get past her to save Clarence?"

"You still got da mirror?"

"Yes." She felt around in her pocket and found the small metal object. It seemed to vibrate ever so slightly, but she couldn't be sure it was the mirror or her imagination. She pulled it out, relieved to find that she could again see its true form through the glamour.

"Da mirror be showin' you da way. Everytin' else… da necklace… da coin… dey just trinkets. You don't need dem, girl."

She opened the mirror. The surface was covered with a fine mist of condensation. She wiped it away with the sleeve of her jacket. The mirror darkened and then a form came into view. "There you are!" she exclaimed as she recognized the Sphinx's shaggy face.

He grinned wider than a Cheshire cat. "See? Da mirror be showin' you what you be needin'. It'll show you where da Griffin be kept." He glanced around and suddenly his smile vanished. "Hmmmm… dis not be good…" Turning back to her, he addressed her sternly. "Da magic is being stirred up in a way most peculiar. I don't like dis. Me thinks you got to hurry."

The mirror darkened once more and the Sphinx vanished. Molly rubbed it again with her sleeve and another face came into view. She gasped. Clarence looked completely defeated, his eyes dull and his feathers tousled and scorched. He raised his eyes up and looked at her. "Molly…" he whispered.

She opened her mouth to respond and the vision in the mirror vanished, leaving her looking at her own reflection. "No!" She rubbed the surface, but the mirror wouldn't show her the Griffin again. "Clarence," she addressed it. "I'll find you. I don't care what happens. I'll find you and get you out of there. Just hang on a little longer. Mr. Cotton needs you desperately."

She shoved the mirror back into her pocket and crawled out from under the bush. The rain was already beginning to lighten as the squall moved away. Blue sky peeked through the storm clouds and was reflected back in the puddles on the sidewalk. She felt a glimmer of hope as she saw it. Tearing back to Mr. Cotton's house, she burst through the door.

"Mr. Cotton!" she cried. "I found another lily." She pointed at a small object lying on the couch. "The shoe! I can see again!"

The old man's face reddened with rage. "What have you done?"

She stopped short. "But... I found another lily... I can see magic again..."

He tried to get up but his legs gave out and he collapsed back on the couch. "I told you it was over. It's too dangerous!"

She pulled the mirror from her pocket. "The Sphinx..." she panted. "He said all I need is right here" She touched a spot over her heart. "He said I can do this."

"No," He argued. "You're just a little girl..."

She interrupted him before he could finish his sentence. "I saw Clarence... in the mirror. He's in real trouble. So are you. I've got to do something."

"Not this," he gasped. "It's better if we..."

"No. I'm going to find Clarence and get him out of there, whether you like it or not."

He sighed. "Well, since you leave me no choice..." He pointed to a cabinet on the far side of the room. "...There's a scroll in the back of the second shelf, behind the DVDs. Can you go get it?"

She retrieved it and brought it over to him. He opened it up carefully on the coffee table and smoothed out the dog-eared corners. It was a map of the city. "Mr. Cotton, no offense, but this map must be at least fifty years old," she remarked.

"Oh, it's a good deal older than that."

She looked at the yellowed parchment. The lines were uneven and wobbly in places, as if drawn with a quill pen. But despite its age she could clearly see the new mall depicted in the center of the map, complete with a tiny illustration of Rymira's fountain. "How did the…" she trailed off and looked at him with a wry smile. "Let me guess. It's a magic map."

He returned her smile weakly and pointed to a place on the map. "Here we are." A red path appeared, marking a route from their current position to a spot on a winding street just a few blocks in from the northwest edge of town. "That's where Euryale lives," He tapped the map three times and it zoomed in to center on the house. Molly saw the main house, as well as a garage and a gardening shed. The entire property was surround-ed by a wall. In addition to large gates in the front, there was a service entrance accessible through a tiny alley behind the garage. He pointed to a spot a little ways away from the back gate that looked like it might be another entrance. "See this? It's the origi-nal gate, but they stopped using it years ago. If you go in through there, you can get inside without being seen. See how it's right next to the garage and pretty overgrown?"

She eyed the tiny opening. The map showed piles of debris on both sides. "Just how accurate is this map?"

"It's a magic map. What do you think?" He touched the gate and a tiny symbol of an open lock appeared. He smiled. "Ah, good. It's not locked." He pointed to the other gates. "She'll have guards posted at the main entrances, but she's most likely forgot-ten about that one."

"Right." Molly was a lot less sure than her answer sounded. "Guards?"

"Yeah, guards." He drew a rectangle around the dark house on the map. The map shifted and zoomed in on the house, now transforming into a blueprint. "Now once you're inside…"

"Wow, that's some map," she remarked. "Good thing you're not a bank robber."

"Bank robber, indeed." He gave her a queer look and changed the subject. "Now, pay attention. This is where the real danger begins."

CHAPTER 30

A half hour later Molly recalled Mr. Cotton's instructions as she rode her bike down the winding street on the last leg of her journey. She passed the front entrance to Miss Gordon's house. There were no guards in sight, but a pair of strange vines grew around and over the posts on either side of a large iron gate. They looked a little like a normal trumpet flower plant, except that the brilliant crimson blooms were much larger and seemed to nod back and forth on their stems regardless of whether there was a breeze or not. They almost appeared like they were looking around, despite the absence of anything that resembled eyes. She regarded them suspiciously and decided to give them a wide berth. As she rounded the corner, she spotted the alley that ran past the back of the property. She dismounted and walked her bike the rest of the way. About halfway down the alley, she located the service entrance—an imposing wrought iron gate flanked on either side by another pair of the same vines.

Just then she heard the sound of footsteps scuffling on the other side of the gate. She ducked behind a trash dumpster two doors away. The gate creaked open and the trumpet flowers began sounding a loud chorus. *"Burglar! Robber! Thief! Trespasser! Murderer!"*

"Quiet, you stupid plants!" A small, wizened old man, almost doubled over by the weight of a large trash can strapped to his back came out of the gate and shook his fist at the vine. "If you're going to be a good watchflower, you need to learn who your friends are."

Another man followed behind, similarly burdened and carrying a rake. "Really, Grandpa," the younger man chuckled. "You know you can't train a watchflower. The blooms only last a day. You'd have to train a new bunch every morning."

The old man grumbled and dumped his trashcan full of leaves and grass clippings into a large plastic bin marked *"Green Waste Only."* The younger man followed suit, and then poked the contents down with his rake. When they went back through the gate the flowers took up the cry again.

"Burglar! Thief! Murderer! Robber! Trespasser!"

Molly waited until the flowers quieted down once more and then tiptoed past them. She suspected they were blind and only reacted to the movement of the gate, but she didn't want to take chances. A few yards past the service entrance, the alley was blocked by a large pile of discarded rubbish too large to fit into the garbage bins. She could just make out a second, rotted wooden gate behind the debris.

She tucked her bike behind a broken down washing machine. For once she was glad her mother could only afford a yard-sale bike—it blended in pretty well with the rest of the junk. She waited a few minutes, listening for the gardeners' return. When she was sure they were not coming back, she set to work opening the gate. Mr. Cotton was right. It was apparent nobody had come through this tiny little door in many years. It wasn't locked but the latch was almost rusted shut. With some effort, she was able to open it just enough for her to shimmy inside.

Hiding in an overgrown lilac bush, she looked around, trying to figure out where the gardeners were. Several large wheelbarrows sat on the driveway, filled with unhappy-looking plants. Molly recognized them immediately. *So, Miss Gordon didn't destroy everything*, she thought hopefully. She caught a glimpse of a drooping sword-shaped dark purple leaf of a faerie lily and was just about to investigate when loud voices erupted from inside the garage. The gardeners were now engaged in a heated debate over where best to plant the flowers. Molly suspected she didn't have much time to cross the yard before the gardeners emerged and ruined her chances for getting into the house unseen. She took a deep breath and sprinted across the broad expansive lawn towards the large imposing house.

As she approached the back door, she recalled Mr. Cotton's instructions:

"Head towards the back door. See? Right here." He touched a spot on the blueprint. *"Don't go inside through there, though. It'll put you right into the kitchen where you're bound to be caught."* He traced his finger along the wall until he found a small window. *"Here's where you should enter— through the basement."*

Slinking around the side of the house, she hid herself in a group of large hydrangea bushes sporting huge clusters of impossibly bright orange flowers. She found the window Mr. Cotton told her about—it was really more of a small opening set a few inches from the ground. She was able to remove the grate that covered it and was just about to stick her head inside when she caught a whiff of something coming from the basement that made her stomach churn. It smelled like a combination of rotten produce, excrement and vomit, with an underlying rank odor that was unlike anything she had ever experienced. She thought about looking around for another way in, but then remembered that Mr. Cotton said the only safe way to enter the house was through the basement. "Probably just where they keep their compost pile," she murmured, "nothing to be afraid of." She was just about to wiggle herself through the small opening when something caught hold of her shirt and pulled her back.

"Wait," a raspy voice hissed.

Molly wheeled around, her heart pounding at the thought that she had been discovered. A small reptilian creature held her shirt with a claw. "Shhhhhhh," it whispered. "Don't move."

CHAPTER 31

Molly sat down in surprise and dismay at the creature's command. She was caught before she even got into the house. It released her and moved into the light where she got a good look at it for the first time. Despite the seriousness of the situation, she had to try really hard to suppress a giggle. She was staring at one of the most ridiculous-looking magical creatures she had ever seen. It looked like a small dinosaur that had been tarred and feathered. White plumage sprouted randomly from odd places all over its body and competed with black reptile scales for space on its head and legs. A brilliant turquoise cockscomb drooped rakishly over to one side of its head, which was attached to its body by a long snakelike neck. Scales covered its tail, which whipped around it as if it had a life of its own. The beast wore a pair of black swim goggles that were modified with tinted lenses to obscure its eyes.

"Ssstupid girl," it hissed and let her go. "You almost made a fatal missssstake."

"Are you… I mean do you… work for Miss Gordon?"

The creature laughed, which sounded like steam escaping from a teakettle. "Me? No. I'd rather be torn to pieces by rabid bugbearssss. I'm only here to make sure you're ssssafe."

She was astonished as she recognized the voice. The past few days began to make sense to her. "The message from the bush… that wasn't from Marcus at all. It was you talking!"

It bobbed its head up and down in agreement. The jerky movement reminded Molly of a chicken, but its voice was pure reptile. It bowed clumsily. "Syrus is my name. I'm sorry, but the message got a little confused. That sneeze sent me three blocks away. You were already at the manticores' den by the time I caught back up with you."

"Wait, the manticores… You're the one who turned them all to stone!"

It exposed a mouthful of small fang-like teeth in something she assumed was a smile. "I'd be lying if I said I did not enjoy doing that. Manticores are nasty horrible beasts."

"So that makes you a stoney-gazer too. Hmmm…" She ran down a mental list of magical creatures until one came to mind. "You're a cockatrice, aren't you? Kind of a cousin to the basilisk." She pointed at the goggles. "And those are Mr. Cotton's. I've seen another pair just like them at his house. How'd you get them?"

The cockatrice nodded. "Jonas Merriweather is an old friend." He touched a claw to the goggles and bowed his head in reverence. "I'm in debt to him for my life." Then he frowned. "You must not go in there. It's a trap!"

"But I have to get inside. I have to save Clarence… and the others," she protested. "Mr. Cotton said the only safe way inside is through the basement."

"He's mistaken. He underestimates Euryale. She knows you're coming and how you plan to enter her house. There's certain death for you if you go in through there."

Molly looked back towards the stinking black hole and moved farther away from it. Her instincts sensed that the cockatrice spoke the truth. "So what do we do?" she whimpered. "That was the only way in."

The cockatrice shrugged. "We leave now and live to hunt another day."

"I can't do that. Mr. Cotton is dying… and it's all my fault!" She tried to hold back her tears. "I have to find Clarence and get him back home. There's no more time!"

"Very well then." It turned and started to go.

"So that's it? You're leaving?"

"Not at all, Miss Molly. I owe my life to Jonas. If this is the only way to save him, then I have no choice but to help you."

Molly relaxed. "So how do we get in?"

"We go through the kitchen. The Griffin is locked upstairs in Euryale's private study."

"H… how do you know that for sure?" she stammered out the question.

"I knew you'd be coming here after you visited the Mermaid," it replied. "I've been waiting for you here since yesterday watching… listening… I've even been in the house and seen the Griffin for myself."

"Is he okay?" she asked, remembering the feather left in her room.

"He's alive… for now. That is all I can really say," the cockatrice answered evasively.

This made her even more determined. "What are we waiting for? Let's get him out of there!" She started to get up.

"Patience, Miss Molly," the cockatrice motioned for her to sit back down. "You're in luck. Euryale left early this morning and will be gone until nightfall. We have time." It started scratching a crude map in the dirt. "Here's the plan. I'll go in first and deal with her guards," it explained slowly in a soothing voice. "When I'm sure it's safe for you, I'll signal you to come inside. Go in through the kitchen and up the back staircase. The second door on the right is her study. You can free the Griffin, but then you should leave. I'll wait in hiding and deal with Euryale later. It's the least I can do to repay my debt to Jonas."

This was much different than Molly's plan. She assumed that everything she had gone through was to prepare her to face Miss Gordon, not to hide in a bush and let someone else fight her battles for her.

"I know what you're thinking," the cockatrice remarked. "You think you have to fight the monster to save the day. But this isn't a fairy tale, Miss Molly. This is real. Anyway Jonas needs the Griffin back a lot more than you need to risk your neck."

She nodded tentatively in agreement. "Okay," she whispered. "What's the signal?"

The cockatrice thought about it for a minute, then threw its head back and let out a loud, high-pitched screech.

Molly winced at the sound. "Oh, that's charming," she remarked dryly. "You could have warned me before doing that so close to my ears."

"Well, you asked," it replied with a hissing chuckle. "Now stay here." With a flip of its tail, it disappeared with a rustle into the hydrangea bush in the direction of the kitchen door.

CHAPTER 32

Molly stayed hidden behind the hydrangea bush for what seemed like an eternity. From the direction of the kitchen she heard voices, a scream and several crashes. At one point it sounded like an entire stack of dishes had been dropped on a ceramic tile floor. There was a door slam, then another, the sound of glass breaking—and then... silence.

Just as she was wondering if the cockatrice had made it to the upstairs study, she heard his screech coming from above her. She looked up and saw an open window, but her view of inside was obscured by billowing curtains. The call came again and this time she saw a flash of a turquoise cockscomb and movement behind the curtains.

She carefully snuck around to the back of the house. The door was slightly open, so she gingerly peeked inside. Broken china lay scattered across the floor and a startled-looking woman stood frozen by the china cabinet. Molly panicked and she almost fled. But after a moment of staring, she realized that the woman wasn't moving. A closer look told her why—the cockatrice had turned her to stone.

She tiptoed through the kitchen, wincing every time a shard of porcelain cracked under her feet. She passed a stone man lying prone with his fingers outstretched towards a door. There was a key in the lock. Loud scratching and snorting sounded from the other side of the door. *That must be the basement,* Molly thought to herself, glad it was locked from the outside. She grabbed the key out of the lock and dropped it into her pocket. The last thing she needed was for someone else to release whatever was hiding behind the door. She felt rather than heard the key clink against the mirror case and it gave her a sense of reassurance.

She spotted another door that was standing ajar. Beyond it she could just make out a narrow staircase in the dim light. She was just wondering if this was the route the cockatrice took, when she saw something at the top of the staircase that answered her question: a pair of familiar goggles. She picked them up and looped the strap around her wrist for safekeeping, planning on returning them when she next saw her new friend.

She counted six doors in the upstairs hall—two on the left and four on the right. Creeping up to the second door on the right, she put her ear against it and listened. She heard the strained breathing of a large animal. *Clarence!* She resisted the sudden urge to throw open the door and storm in, Instead, she slowly pushed it open and poked her head inside.

The study was dark—All but one of the windows were covered with heavy thick curtains that blocked the light. The far one was open, its curtains swaying in the breeze. Molly recognized this as where the cockatrice called from only a few minutes before. As her eyes became accustomed to the dim light, she noticed an enormous iron cage in the center of the room. Clarence lay sprawled out inside, wearing a heavy collar tightly around his neck. He was either asleep or unconscious, his breath coming in long, heavy gasps. She looked around for the cockatrice and saw his unmistakable silhouette half-concealed behind a large armchair. She relaxed and entered the room, her footfall silenced by the thick carpet.

"Syrus," she said in a loud whisper, "I found your goggles. I don't suppose you meant to lose them…" her voice trailed off, as she got closer. Something wasn't right. The cockatrice stared directly at her, but its gaze would never turn another person to stone. She touched its head, felt the soft feathers and shiny scales now turned to hard granite and realized it had made a terrible mistake. "Oh, Syrus," she muttered. "You were wrong. Miss Gordon's been here all along!"

CHAPTER 33

Molly wheeled around just in time to see Miss Gordon emerge from behind the door and flip on the light switch. The room was bathed in bright light. Molly paled and ducked behind the armchair.

"Well, well, well," the substitute said in mock surprise. "What do we have here?" She strode to the center of the room and positioned herself directly between Molly and the cage and addressed its occupant. "Why Clarence, It looks like a second nasty little thief has tried to break into my home today." She patted the Griffin on his hindquarters. Even in sleep he flinched at her touch. "What do you think we should do with her?"

"I'm not afraid of you," Molly growled through clenched teeth. "I'm here to take Clarence home."

"Did you hear that, Griffin? The little thief wants to kidnap you away from me," Miss Gordon addressed him with the same unbelievable tone of shock. She deftly reached into the cage and plucked a feather from his wing and used the quill to clean a bit of dirt from under one of her perfectly manicured fingernails. When she was finished she dropped the feather and ground it under her heel. "Now I ask you, how do you suppose she's going to do that, especially after I've already dealt with one trespasser?" She nodded at the stone cockatrice.

Molly shivered. For a moment her fear and self-doubt returned. *I'm going to die*, she thought. Then she remembered the words of the Sphinx:

"Da mirror be showin' you what you be needin'."

She reached into her pocket and carefully took out the mirror case. It seemed so tiny now, barely larger than a regular compact. Molly had no idea how she could possibly use it without being turned to stone in the process, but it was all she had left. She opened it up and fit the two halves together. They formed a seamless surface. She was ready.

"The cockatrice really had no chance, the poor thing," Miss Gordon continued. "At least, not after it took off those stupid goggles..." She chuckled. "The foolish creature actually thought it could turn me to stone..."

Of course! Molly looked at the goggles strung around her wrist and silently thanked her lucky stars for stumbling across them and having the good sense to pick them up. She loosened the straps as far as they would go and put them over her eyes. The cockatrice's head was much narrower than hers so the straps were uncomfortably tight, but the eyepieces covered her eyes well, owing for the unfortunate creature's disproportionately large eyes. She picked up the mirror and rose from her hiding place to face Miss Gordon...

...Euryale the Gorgon, she corrected herself when she faced the monster. Her former substitute teacher had undergone a horrible transformation. Instead of the attractive, slim, blonde woman Molly knew from school, her teacher was now the hideous monster she remembered from the vision in Rymira's mirror. Euryale's eyes, although hypnotizing before, now burned with such fire that even with the protection of the cockatrice's goggles, Molly still had to look away.

Euryale advanced. "You made a fatal mistake, Molly Stevens. Now you and everyone close to you will pay the price. As soon as I am finished with you, I'll make good on my promise. The Griffin is as good as dead. Your family is already under my enchantment—their hearts will continue to beat slower and slower until they finally stop." She took a step forward and her eyes glowed. "As for you... *You'll make a nice addition to my collection.*"

"You… you turned Syrus to stone!"

Miss Gordon laughed. "Yes, my dear. And you are next. She lifted her gaze and Molly found she could not look away…

"Wait for it, girl… when dat monster turn dat stoney gaze on you, use da mirror!" The Sphinx' voice echoed in her mind.

Euryale's eyes began to glow bright yellow. Through the goggles, Molly saw the change as clearly as a gun being cocked. She raised the mirror in front of her face just before the gorgon unleashed the full force of her gaze. The mirror expanded into a reflective shield, enveloping Molly like a cocoon and protecting her. There was a flash and a terrible cry from Miss Gordon as her magic was turned back upon her. The mirror flamed and Molly dropped it to the floor. The shield disappeared and Molly came face to face with the gorgon. But all that remained of the great and terrible Euryale was a column of black ash. As Molly watched in wonder, a gust of wind from the open window began to blow it away.

Molly removed the goggles and bent down to retrieve the mirror. As she watched, it shrank and then split along the seam, falling into the two, hinged halves. But now the surface was pitted and blackened. It could never be used as a mirror again. She couldn't bear to discard it, so she folded it up and carefully returned it to her pocket.

Stepping over to the cockatrice, she sadly stroked its stone feathers. She took the goggles and strapped them over her friend's cold, unseeing eyes. A tear rolled down her cheek and dripped from her chin onto the top of the cockatrice's head. She stepped over to the curtains and threw open the first set. The room was filled with light but the inner curtains still blocked the sun. She tore those away and moved to the second window, where she did the same. At the third window a small movement caught her attention and she plucked a tiny white fluffy feather from where it was caught in the window. She removed the mirror case from her pocket once more and laid the small feather in between the two halves of the mirror. It was all she had to remember the cockatrice by. Then she ripped away the inner curtains and sunlight flooded the room, falling directly on the stone creature. It gave a shudder and she thought she heard a sigh as it crumbled into dust.

CHAPTER 34

Molly was never sure afterwards whether it was the sudden sunlight that woke Clarence or if he was under a spell that vanished when the gorgon was destroyed. Whatever the case, when she turned back towards him he was awake and looking at her with sleepy emerald eyes. "Ahem," he croaked. "If you are done trashing the room, can we do something about getting me out of this cage?"

"Okay, let me see if I can find a key or something."

"She keeps them over there. In her desk."

She rummaged around in the drawers while the Griffin tapped his claws impatiently on the hard floor. Finally she located a large ring of assorted padlock keys in the bottom of the last one. The first key didn't fit, but after several tries with others similar in size and shape, she found the right one. The lock turned with a loud click and she opened the door.

He wobbled out on unsteady legs. "Now, if you would be so kind and get this blasted thing off my neck." She found a tiny gold key on the ring that fit the collar and it dropped to the floor with a thump. He turned his head from side to side and stretched, "Ah... Much better." He extended his wings and shook himself, almost knocking Molly over in the process. One of his wings tipped over a cabinet full of curios and it landed with a crash. "Oops," he remarked coldly.

"I wonder..." She knelt in front of the ruined cabinet and sifted through the broken glass until with a shout she lifted up a small wooden box. She showed him the contents—an amber pendant, a golden coin and three crystal vials of a dark purple juice. "Ugh," he snorted with disgust, "that coin reeks of that rotten Cornelius. Tell me that fool Barnaby didn't send you to seek him out, did he?" He muttered several colorful insults pertaining to the Leprechaun under his breath.

She smiled but said nothing.

His big green eyes twinkled when he saw the vials. "Barnaby will be happy to see those," he remarked. "It's been fifty years since the last time he ran out of lily juice—and that time was only for a day. I can't imagine what's it's been like for him to be without magic for this long."

Molly suddenly remembered why she was there. "Oh my God! Mr. Cotton! Clarence, we've got to get back to him now! He's terribly hurt!" She explained the wound and how it was poisoned.

He looked worried, but shook his great head. "We can't go just yet. Euryale may be gone forever, but some of her more despicable minions are still around. We can't leave any of her prisoners here, even for a minute. We have to find them all—every last one. Barnaby wouldn't want it any other way even if it meant... Well... you know."

She opened her mouth to protest, but then thought better of it. He was right about Mr. Cotton. The old man would rather die than allow any of the magical creatures to remain here. Her best bet was to help Clarence find them all, as quickly as possible.

He tucked his wings tightly against his chest and squeezed through the door. "Coming?" he called impatiently over his shoulder.

She followed closely behind. Euryale was dead, but they were up against a greater foe now: time. She was worried—she had no idea how fast the poison would travel through Barnaby's frail body. They would just have to hurry and trust that they would be able to get back in time to save him.

Clarence appeared less concerned with the time and insisted that they conduct a thorough search of the house. They moved through the upstairs rooms first, looking for creatures that might be caged. In the sleeping porch they found a small birdcage containing several pixies trying to make a home out of a weather-beaten birdhouse. Molly freed them and asked them to fly to Mr. Cotton's house and deliver the news that Euryale was dead. They looked a little nervously at the large Griffin and quickly flew away.

In the end Clarence was right to suggest searching the entire house. They released three silent nightingales from a cage in a closet and a moping phoenix chained to a perch in the den. There was a basket full of parched salamanders on the hearth next to the living room fireplace. "She used them as fire starters," he remarked. "Salamanders are better than matches."

"How could she?" Molly exclaimed as she released them. "You're all free now," she said to them. "Go home!"

There were lots of unpleasant discoveries to be made as well. While exploring the hallway that led into the conservatory, they came across two long rapier-like spiral horns in an umbrella stand. Clarence bowed his head sadly. "Unicorns," he said. "These were two of maybe a handful left in the Nine Realms." He sniffed them. "Might as well bring those along," he added, "We might need them. The horns are the only cure against the poison from the sting of a manticore. Leaving them here would just be an insult to the lives that were taken."

He didn't elaborate any further but Molly understood. She grabbed the horns and looked around for something to wrap them in. Settling on a throw draped across a couch and a cord used to tie back curtains, she was able to fashion a crude sling. She threw the bundle across her back and hurried to catch up with Clarence. He nodded towards a shelf where a family of brownies was stuck in a fishbowl. She tipped the bowl into her cupped hands and carefully lifted them up to her shoulder. They perched there like small brown birds, twittering their heartfelt thanks in high-pitched voices.

In this roundabout manner the pair finally reached the kitchen, trailed by a motley group of rescued creatures. Clarence stopped in front of the door to the basement. Something still snarled and growled, but Molly was no longer afraid. In fact, after defeating the gorgon, she felt pretty invincible. Struggling to get the key out of her pocket, she stumbled and knocked the arm off the stone man lying on the floor. "Oops."

The Griffin shook his head and rolled his eyes. "Well, I suppose we can't leave them like this. You know the drill." Together they tore open the blinds. Sunlight fell on the unfortunate victims of the cockatrice and they crumbled into dust almost immediately.

He nodded to the basement door. "Let's get this over with." There was a low growl in response. Clarence flattened his ears and roared, causing the group of rescued creatures to scatter in fear. Whatever was on the other side of the door backed away and stopped moving. The Griffin put a talon up to his face to signal silence and nodded his head. Molly deftly fit the key into the door and opened it.

They were immediately assaulted by the same horrible stench from the basement grate—only a hundred times stronger. It was enough to make Molly's eyes water and bile rise in her throat. She gagged and stepped back from the yawning darkness, but not before she caught sight of a pair of malevolent red eyes shining like lights at the bottom of the stairs.

CHAPTER 35

Clarence sniffed the air and wrinkled his nose in disgust. "Trolls," he spat. "It's a good thing you didn't come in through the basement. They would have torn you apart."

Molly shuddered, recalling how close she had been to doing that very thing. "Yeah. Good thing," she agreed. She held her nose. "We don't have to go in there, do we?"

"I'm afraid so," he growled. "Euryale kept many of us down there, guarded by those trolls. Once they figure out she's dead... well, she was the only thing keeping them from eating everyone in their care." He sounded grim.

"How many trolls do you think there are?"

"Hmmmmm. Two... No... Three." He sniffed again and sneezed. "Yep, there's three trolls." He examined his talons, frowning at the remnants of chipped purple nail polish that still clung to them. "Piece of cake." His eyes had a steely glint to them.

It was only then that she remembered that one of his claws had been sliced off at the knuckle, leaving a stump caked with dried blood.

He caught her stare. "Well, I suppose it's a small loss in comparison to what could have happened," he remarked, nodding towards the horns strapped to her back. "At least I'm still alive."

She nodded in agreement. She couldn't think of anything else to say.

He moved to the door. "Stay here. It's not a place for little girls. I'll call you when I'm done with the trolls."

"Are you sure? You're hurt."

He frowned. "I'll live. Besides, I could use a little excitement after being cooped up. How can I go back with my head held high if it were known that you did all of the work?" With that he raced down the stairs with his tail lashing out behind him.

Moments later, she heard an awful clamor and three inhuman howls as Clarence made short work of the trolls. Then he called her down. "You still have that key ring, don't you?"

She jingled it. "Yeah. It's right here."

"Good. We'll need it."

She took off the bundle and set the brownies down on the counter. "You'll be safer up here, little guys." They chirped and made a beeline for a plate of chocolate chip cookies.

Stepping into the doorway, she found a light switch and flicked it on. The stairs were covered in some kind of slimy filth that made them slippery and treacherous. At one point there had been a handrail, but it was chewed to a stump long ago. She tread carefully on the far edges of the stairs where the slime wasn't quite as thick. As she descended, the odor intensified until it made her eyes water. When she reached the bottom she fought to keep from throwing up at what she saw.

In addition to being housed in a confined space with trolls— in itself a horrible enough fate—the unfortunate prisoners were held in filthy conditions with no light or fresh air. Fur was matted and caked; feathers were ragged and falling out. Most of the creatures had open, weeping sores and some had gone blind from malnutrition. Several had died in their cages and were left to rot. Clarence sat atop the bodies of three trolls. He looked furious.

She stepped over to the first cage. A sad-looking harpy eyed her hopefully from within its rusty prison. Its wings and body were slimy with something that looked like raw petroleum. "Troll spit," Clarence growled.

Molly pulled the key ring out and began sorting through it until she found a promising key. She fit it into the lock and it popped open. She addressed the occupant. "How long have you been down here?"

"Six years... I think," The harpy croaked. "My sister and I came from Isla Rubos... in the Sixth Realm."

"Where is she now?"

The harpy looked mournfully towards a dark corner. Molly pointed her flashlight in that direction and saw a large pile of disjointed bones. Most of them looked gnawed. "Clarence!" she shrieked.

The Griffin heard her cry and turned his attention towards the circle of light from her flashlight. The hackles on his neck rose. "I knew it was bad, but I had no idea!" he roared. "There must have been hundreds kept in this hellhole. Let's hurry and get the rest of them out of here."

While Molly continued fitting keys to padlocks, Clarence had a different approach. He simply ripped the doors off the cages with his strong claws, freeing three creatures to every one that Molly released. When they were through, there was a pile of twisted metal on the floor.

Each creature had a different reaction to freedom. Some rushed out of the basement and fled up the stairs to where there was fresh air and sunlight. Some milled around a little, waiting for instruction from their rescuers, whom they now identified as the new authority figures in their lives. Still others sat in their cages, completely unable to accept that their suffering was finally over, until they were coaxed, threatened or simply forcibly removed and taken upstairs.

CHAPTER 36

When all the creatures were free, Clarence and Molly returned to the cellar one final time. "This house must be completely destroyed," Clarence muttered. "The pain and suffering that's happened here makes it the perfect breeding ground for dark magic." He gathered up the bodies of the trolls and threw them in the pile of refuse in the center of the room.

"Destroyed?"

"Yes. Fire will be the best way, I think. There's enough stuff down here to burn. All we need is a way to ignite it."

"I'll get some matches." Without waiting for an answer, Molly ran upstairs. An informal group had assembled in the kitchen, awaiting further instructions. She called out to them as she hunted through the room. "I think Clarence is going to blow up the house, so you all need to get out of here."

"But where can we go?" a faun asked her.

Molly stopped short. She hadn't thought of that. In her haste to save Clarence and Mr. Cotton, it never occurred to her that there would be others, or where they should go. Considering her options, she settled on the only choice. "Mr. Cotton's waiting for you right now at his house. He'll help you." It was stretching the truth a little—she didn't know if he was even still alive, let alone in any condition to help this many refugees from Euryale's prison. But it would get them out of harm's way for now and they could work on permanent homes later. "Some of you already know the way to his house," she continued, her eyes making contact with the faun who nodded. "Those who do, please lead the others and help those who are unable to travel themselves."

She started to leave but then snapped her fingers as she remembered something important. "Oh. I almost forgot. There are several wheelbarrows full of plants stolen from Mr. Cotton's garden out by the garage. Please take them back with you—it will mean a lot to him."

There were several affirming nods and the group started to break up and move slowly towards the back door. Molly continued searching. "You've got to be kidding me! This has to be the only kitchen in the entire world without matches."

Clarence's voice floated upstairs. "What's taking so long? I could've started a fire by rubbing two pencils together in less time."

"I can't find any matches!"

"Well, hurry up. We're running out of time."

Molly frantically pulled a little too hard on the last drawer, spilling the contents all over the floor. She knelt and started sifting through the collection of kitchen junk—coupons, used birthday candles, ketchup packets... It seemed like everything anyone could possibly ever collect was in this drawer... except matches. "What am I going to do now?" she groaned.

A tiny voice buzzed above her. "Excuse me, miss..."

Molly looked up. A tiny glowing boy hovered a few inches in front of her face. "I told you all to get out of here," she snapped.

"I know that, miss... But I was wondering if I could be of assistance..."

"Unless you can materialize some matches for me, I doubt you can help."

"I don't have any matches..." He spread his fingers and his hands ignited with blue flames. "...But I don't exactly need them. You see, miss, I'm a fire sprite."

"A fire sprite?" she repeated.

"Yes. I thought perhaps, if you'd like, my boys and I could start whatever fires you might need."

She grinned. "Oh please! That would be wonderful."

He bowed in midair. "It'd be my honor, Miss. We all owe you for what you've done here." He whistled loudly and four more glowing boys appeared. They bowed in succession as their leader named them off. "This here's Crackle, Ember, Fizzle and Pop. You can call me Tinder."

Molly wasn't quite sure what to make of the ragtag crew. They had a mischievous quality about them that seemed a little outside the law. She suspected that the opportunity to burn the house down was just as appealing to the sprites as being helpful. *But beggars can't be choosy*, she decided and gave a short bow. "I'm Molly. Nice to meet you. Thanks for helping me."

"No problem, little lady," Fizzle assured her. He rubbed his hands together excitedly, causing green sparks to rain to the floor. "Okay kids, let's have some fun…"

Molly held a hand up. "Hold on. We have to make sure everyone gets outside, first. I don't want anyone hurt."

"Yeah, Fizzle," Tinder reprimanded him with a cuff on the ear. "Don't get carried away."

"Oh, yeah… right," the sprite mumbled.

Another groaned. "But that's no fun…"

"Quiet, Pop!" Crackle hissed, punching him in the arm, causing orange sparks to sputter.

"Hey, what'd you do that for?" Pop griped. He took a swing at Crackle and missed.

Tinder whistled again and they snapped to attention. "Gentlemen! We're here to help Miss Molly. That means we wait until everyone's safely outside."

Molly stood up and addressed the room. "Everyone, you have about five minutes before this place goes up in flames." She eyed the sprites. "Personally, I plan to be out of here in three." She went back into the basement, where Clarence was just putting the last touches on a large pile of cardboard boxes, broken furniture and rotten paper.

"Well? Did you find matches?" he asked without turning around.

"Not exactly. But I think I've got something better."

He glanced over his shoulder and noticed the group of glowing orbs buzzing around her head. "*Sprites?*"

She cringed. "Yeah, well I couldn't find any matches and they said they'd be honored to help after all we'd done."

The Griffin narrowed his eyes suspiciously. "Fine. But no funny business," he addressed them.

"No worries, Mister Griffin, sir. We're just helping Miss Molly," Tinder replied. He floated around the room. "Hmmmmm… lots of dry wood here. And troll spit."

Crackle started to giggle. "Troll spit… Awesome!"

Molly signaled to Tinder. "What's so great about troll spit?"

Pop broke in before he could reply. "Trolls is highly flammable, Ma'am. Better 'n' gasoline, if you ask me…"

"She didn't," Tinder snapped and turned back to Molly. "Anyway, he's right." He broke into a grin. "This place is gonna go up like a Christmas tree on Burn Day!"

She looked at him curiously. "Burn Day? What's…" She noticed Clarence glaring at her and stopped herself in mid-sentence. "Nevermind. You can tell me later."

"Maybe we should just figure out something else," Clarence grumbled. "I don't like this…"

Tinder flew over and hovered in front of the Griffin. "We can handle this just fine. You don't have anything to worry about."

"Yeah," Ember added. "Fire's our specialty. There ain't nobody in the Nine Realms that knows more 'bout setting fires than Tinder."

"Somehow that doesn't surprise me," Clarence muttered. "Come on, Molly. Let's get out of here before the Matchbox Brothers get carried away."

He started up the stairs with Molly close behind. Tinder followed them as far as the top of the stairs. "Good luck, Miss Molly and Mr. Griffin. We'll see you again real soon." He turned and with a whoop, soared back down into the basement. There were four answering shouts. Molly glanced back and saw that the sprites were already starting to ignite the walls with streams of colored flames from their fingers.

"I knew it!" Clarence cried. "Those rotten little punks! Come on, we've got to get out of here. The place is going to blow!"

"Wait!" She ducked across the room and grabbed the sling with the unicorn horns. "I can't leave these."

They had barely cleared the doorway before the basement exploded with a flash of light and a loud boom. Molly was thrown into the air and landed in an unconscious heap on the lawn. She came to with a fit of coughing and saw Clarence standing over her. "I knew they were trouble," he snorted. "Never trust a sprite."

She looked up and saw smoke billowing from the basement and downstairs windows. "Yeah, I'll try to remember that," she groaned.

The faint sound of approaching sirens screamed in the distance. "I think we should probably get out of here before there's any more trouble. How about a lift?" he suggested.

She gave him a weak smile and wheezed. "That would be great."

The Griffin picked her up carefully in his talons and extended his wings. He gave a few experimental hops to adjust his take off for the extra weight. Then he leapt into the air and circled the house twice. Molly noted with satisfaction the orange flames beginning to lick the walls of the living room as thick smoke poured out of the windows. Then with a flip of his tail, Clarence turned east and headed home.

CHAPTER 37

Molly and Clarence descended out of a cloud directly over Mr. Cotton's house and landed in the backyard. There was a crowd of animals and other magical creatures gathered on the back porch. As soon as they touched the ground a faun approached them. Molly recognized it as the one she talked to in Miss Gordon's kitchen.

"You told us to come here. So we came, but I don't think anyone's home," he bleated. Some of the others gathered around and nodded.

Clarence turned and looked at her as she slid from his back. "I think we need to get inside right away. I don't like the looks of this." He padded up to the back porch and slid a claw into the locked French doors. They opened with a soft click and he disappeared inside. After a moment, he returned and beckoned to Molly to join him. "Only you. Everyone else stays outside," he whispered.

She ducked inside, fearing the worst. Mr. Cotton lay on the couch, his skin pale and his breathing barely perceivable. Constable Taralinda sat at his side. She looked up when they approached. "Oh, good. I see you're back." She wasn't smiling.

"Is he going to be okay?" Molly dared to ask.

"It was close, but now that Clarence is here, he might have a chance."

Molly let out a sigh of relief. It was short-lived, however, when she saw the grim expression on the Griffin's face.

"What's wrong?"

He shook his head. "I can't heal this. This magic is too strong. It's beyond my powers."

"No!" Molly cried. "He said you could heal him. He said you were the only one."

"That old coot always did overestimate my power," Clarence replied, large tears running down his feathered cheeks. "I told him before I'm not a unicorn…" He stopped. "Wait! A unicorn! Molly, do you still have those horns?"

She blinked. "Yeah… I left them outside on the porch, but…"

"Go get them!"

She tore across the room and shoved open the French doors, nearly knocking over a brownie with his nose glued to the window. The sling still lay where she set it down on the steps. She grabbed the larger of the two horns and ran back inside. "Here," she panted as she handed the horn to the Elf.

"He's a lucky man," Taralinda commented as she drew a small utility knife from her jacket and unfolded a diamond file. She unwrapped the bandage from the old man's leg, revealing a place that was swollen and black. Filing a small amount of powder from the horn, she sprinkled it on the ugly wound.

Almost immediately, the black poison receded and the color began to return to the old man's face. The swelling diminished and the weeping sore scabbed over and started to heal. Within a few minutes, the sting was completely gone, leaving only a silvery white scar on his shin. Mr. Cotton coughed and opened his eyes. "Wha… what happened?" He looked around and caught sight of Clarence. "Oh, Constable Taralinda! You found him!"

She shook her head and rolled her eyes. "It wasn't me. Regulations, you know. I couldn't get involved. It was the girl."

"Molly?"

Molly approached the couch. "I told you I'd find Clarence," she grinned. "By the way, how does he look?"

Mr. Cotton squinted and shook his head sadly. "Like a dog. I suppose the Sight is gone for me now, isn't it?"

Taralinda nodded. "You went against my specific orders. You know the rules. It would be one thing if the lilies were here, but they were all destroyed. I can't justify a trip to the Fifth Realm to procure more... at least not until the council rules on this."

Mr. Cotton looked as if someone had let the air out of him. "I understand," he softly whispered.

Molly stepped up and pulled the vials of purple liquid from her pocket. "I found these. Maybe they'll help." She turned them over to the Elf.

Taralinda peered at the vials. "This is a tincture made from *Zephranthes occulanium*. Child, where did you get these?"

"Miss Gor... I mean Euryale's house. They were the same color as the juice on my fingers... so I thought..."

"You guessed correctly," Taralinda replied. "This will restore the Sight, at least for a little while."

"Good thing, too," Clarence muttered. "There's a pretty large crowd of refugees from Euryale's House of Horrors out back. They're going to need some attention."

Mr. Cotton sat up and reached for the vial. "Constable... may I? Clarence... the animals... they need me!"

Reluctantly Taralinda handed over the vials. "I suppose you will need these. I guess we'll have to figure out what to do when this runs out, maybe I can get a special permit to the Fifth Realm?"

"Constable Taralinda?" Molly spoke up. "The lilies weren't destroyed. We brought most of them back with us." She pointed towards the back of the house. "They're outside."

The constable broke out into a wide grin and addressed Mr. Cotton. "The specifics of your license are clear—as long as the lilies are growing on your property, you have been granted unrestricted permission to use them to perform the work you have been contracted to do." She paused and her voice softened. "What are you waiting for? Go help them."

Mr. Cotton applied the tincture to both his eyes and his ears. He shut his eyes and grimaced for a few moments. When he opened them he had a look of concern on his face. "Clarence! Your feathers!"

"Nothing a good molt won't fix."

The old man smiled. "It's good to hear your voice again, my friend. I was so worried…"

"I'll be fine. But the others…"

Mr. Cotton got up carefully from the couch. Molly could tell he was still a little weak in the knees, but he would soon make a full recovery. He hobbled across the room towards the French doors. "Molly, are you coming?"

"Right behind you." She started to follow him but her way was blocked by the Elf.

"I'm sorry, child, but I cannot let you pass. Although Barnaby is free to go back to doing the work he loves, I'm afraid there is still your crime to deal with."

"My crime?" Molly was momentarily confused. "What did I do?"

Taralinda sighed. "Really? Don't play stupid. You knew perfectly well that you were not to ever touch the lilies again. Yet, as soon as your Sight faded, you stole another one."

"But… I mean Mr. Cotton said…"

"I know what he said. I was watching. He told you specifically not to touch those lilies again. Even if it meant his…"

"…His death," Molly finished. "But I couldn't let him die. And I couldn't leave Clarence…"

"I'm not saying what you did was wrong. But you broke several rules, the least of which was going against a directive from a constable from the Magic Compliance Committee. There has to be repercussions."

Clarence and Mr. Cotton noticed the conversation and returned. "What's going on?" Mr. Cotton asked.

"The girl. She broke the law. I'm going to have to use the Spell of Forgetfulness."

"But she won't remember anything. Not me… not Clarence…" the old man pleaded.

Taralinda bowed her head. "I'm sorry. But it must be so. You've caused too much disturbance to her life as it is. You can't expect her to continue living with one foot in each of our worlds. Trust me. It's really for the best. You know what the Council will do if they find out she's gone against their directive and used magic again."

Molly looked up in alarm. "What are you talking about? Are you going to take away my Sight?" She kneeled in front of the Elf. "Please. Don't."

"Child, you don't know what you are saying. We just want your life to be as it was…"

"No!" Molly cried. "You don't understand how awful my life was before… before Mr. Cotton and those flowers. I had nothing." She looked up at the constable with tears in her eyes. "Please… Now I have something to look forward to every day. I feel like I am doing something good… helping out… making a difference. For the first time I feel like I matter."

The Elf looked at Barnaby with a puzzled expression.

He scratched the back of his head and flushed red with embarrassment. "Molly's very popular with our guests. She has a way of knowing what each one needs," he confessed. "I've never seen anything like it. It's like she understands them. Marcus never would have recovered as fast without her. She's a regular little Florence Nightingale. I couldn't ask for a more caring helper and she's not afraid of much. Heck, she faced a manticore completely unarmed and unprepared."

Taralinda looked shocked and turned to the little girl crumpled at her feet. "Is this true, child? You looked upon the face of the man-eater?"

Molly rose to her knees. "Well," she hesitated. "I was really scared, but I remembered what Mr. Cotton told me about showing no fear. It was hard though, when he started talking about how he was going to eat me."

Taralinda looked at Barnaby. "She understands the speech of the animals?"

He nodded. "Most of them… At least those she's encountered."

The constable studied Molly for a moment with an expression that was almost impossible to read. "Hmmmm… the lily juice doesn't grant the power to understand magic speech—only the ability to hear it." She gave the old man a sideways glance. "You ought to know this."

He looked down at his feet. "Maybe…"

Taralinda shook her head and broke into a grin. "Very well. If this is what you want, you may continue your apprenticeship."

Molly jumped to her feet. "Did you hear that Clarence? I'm going to be helping Mr. Cotton for good!"

Clarence rolled his big green eyes. "Oh, brother. I suppose this means I'm stuck listening to your chatter on a daily basis…" He looked sharply at Mr. Cotton. "She's not moving in, is she?"

Mr. Cotton laughed. "And have to share a bathroom with you? Goodness no, Clarence! I wouldn't dream of putting her through that." He turned to the Elf. "Constable, what should we do when the magic wears off next time?"

Taralinda drew an object out of her jacket. It looked like a narrow pen, except that it didn't seem to have a point to write with. She pulled on each end and it lengthened into a slim rod that was about eighteen inches long.

"Is that a…?" Molly began.

"Yes, it's a wand," Taralinda replied. "Standard issue. I'm afraid it's a little drab for my tastes, but it's regulation." She touched the wand to each of Molly's ears. "Now close your eyes and hold very still," she cautioned." I don't want to poke you." She tapped each eyelid in turn very lightly.

Molly felt a warmth on her eyes, as if someone was holding a candle right in front of each of them. Her ears tingled slightly, but it wasn't the angry buzzing she associated with the lily potion. "When can I open my eyes?"

"Now, if you like. Elven magic is a little different than plant magic."

Molly opened her eyes and looked around. "Yeah, a lot less painful," she agreed.

"And a little more potent. You will be able to see and hear magic folk for good, now. You'll never have to worry about it wearing off." She looked at Mr. Cotton. "What about you? Are you ready to give up the lilies?"

He grumbled. "For Pete's sake, why didn't you tell me you could do this earlier? You sat there and let me think my Sight was gone forever. Then you let me put that blasted plant juice in my eyes?"

Taralinda smirked. "You needed to be taught a lesson. And I'll admit, it was fun watching you squirm when you thought you'd be like every other mortal for the rest of your life."

"Hmmmph. Well… get on with it then."

She touched his eyes and ears with her wand. "Now, there's something else you should know. I didn't just restore your Sight because I'm a nice person. Elven magic has another side effect— you can now see past the borders and enter the Nine Realms."

Barnaby sat down in shock. "The Nine Realms? No human has ever been allowed past the borders…"

"Well, circumstances have changed. No human—let alone a little girl—has pulled off such a daring offensive and rescued so many of our citizens in one operation. This has not escaped the Council's attention. They request your presence at their next meeting." She tapped the wand and it shrank back to the size of a pen and she tucked it away in her pocket. "As for you… Jonas… I mean Barnaby…" She paused and looked curiously at him. "What should I be calling you anyway?"

"It's true that I haven't gone by Jonas in many years because of Euryale. But I think I like the new name."

"Very well, Barnaby Cotton." She straightened herself up. "I'll be taking my leave, now. I have quite a long report to write when I get back." She gave Molly a salute. "Molly Stevens, you've done a great service to the Nine Realms. Thank you." With that she disappeared with a pop.

Clarence climbed up on the couch. "Well kids, that was fun, but I think it's time for my program." He looked around, as if noticing the condition of the house for the first time. Hey Barnaby? Where's the TV?"

CHAPTER 38

The next day Molly came home from school and headed straight over to Mr. Cotton's house, where she knocked on the door. Nobody answered, so she let herself in quietly and deposited her bookbag on the table next to the door. "Hello? Anyone there?" When there was no response, she wandered into the living room and sat down on the couch to wait. After a few minutes, she heard voices—Mr. Cotton's cheerful chattering and Clarence's dry commentary. The pair came in from the garden.

Mr. Cotton had almost made a full recovery. He still limped, but he had wasted no time restoring the wheelbarrows full of plants back to their beds, if the dirt and grass ground into his knees and the leaves in his hair were any indication. A trowel handle stuck haphazardly out of his back pocket.

Clarence looked as if he had taken a well-deserved bath. There was a large bandage over his missing claw and the others were freshly painted a shocking shade of electric green. His feathers were smooth and his fur shone brightly. Aside from the missing claw, there was no indication of his confinement except for a faint crease around his neck where the feathers were marred. It was the mark from the collar he had worn during his incarceration. Molly figured he didn't need to be reminded of that unpleasant time so she made a silent promise not to ever mention this slight imperfection to him. She was sure the ragged feathers would be gone after the next molt anyway.

The old man was the first to notice her. "Oh, good," he exclaimed. "You're here." He hobbled over and plopped down clumsily into an armchair positioned across from the sofa. A cloud of dust blew into the air and dust motes danced in the sunlight.

Clarence padded softly over and sat on his haunches next to Mr. Cotton's chair. Molly scooted over as far as she could to make room for the Griffin in his favorite spot, but he dismissed her effort with a wave of his talon. His green nails gleamed iridescently, matching the shine of his blue-black feathers. He looked contented and happy.

"Clarence told me about the cockatrice," Mr. Cotton began, looking uncomfortably into his lap. "I'm sorry."

She nodded, allowing a tear to spring into her eyes. "He… he saved my life. More than once."

"You were very brave and very smart to figure out how to defeat Euryale," he added. "Not many people could have done that."

"I guess," she sniffed.

"There's something I've been meaning to ask. How on earth did you manage to get her to look into a mirror without being turned to stone yourself?"

"Well, all I can say was that I was really lucky," she answered. "When I came upstairs thinking the coast was clear, I found Syrus's goggles and picked them up to return them to him."

"Ahhhh…" Mr. Cotton sighed. "I remember making those because he had a fear that he would be turned to stone himself. At the time I indulged him, thinking he was just being paranoid. Now I wonder… Was it paranoia? Or premonition?" He looked wistfully at a dust mote floating in a shaft of sunlight. "So you picked up the goggles—did Syrus ever explain them to you?"

"No. He just said that he was indebted to you for making them for him. I thought at first they just worked the other way around—to prevent the cockatrice from hurting others. But then

Euryale told me she was only able to turn him to stone once he took the goggles off."

"So you put them on, which prevented Euryale from turning you to stone, and then held up the Mermaid's mirror and turned her gaze back on herself. Very ingenious," he congratulated her. "Well done!"

Molly pulled the amber pendant from inside her shirt and unhooked the chain. She ran her fingers over the smooth stone and the filigree setting. She held it up and a shaft of sunlight caught the stone and set it on fire. "I guess I won't be needing this anymore," she said solemnly, handing it to him.

"Nonsense," He scoffed and waved her away. "Now is the time to wear it proudly as a symbol of everything you have been through and accomplished. I think the Sphinx would want it that way, don't you?"

"I know he'll be very proud of you, Molly," Clarence agreed. "I've known that cat for a very long time and he's always had a soft spot for those who go up against great odds to help their friends. He will no doubt enjoy hearing your story when you see him next." The great Griffin's eyes became moist so he quickly cleared his throat and changed the subject. "Anyway, it's good you're back. There's a lot of cleaning up that needs to be done around here," he said gruffly. "Starting with that contemptuous flying monkey! He got a hold of a banana somewhere and has the most revolting boils on his..."

"Clarence!" Mr. Cotton snapped. We do not talk about our guests in such a manner."

Molly stuck her hand in her front pocket and frowned. "Hey, it's gone!" she exclaimed.

"What?" the Griffin asked.

"My lucky coin. The one Cornelius gave me."

Clarence snorted. "He's taken it back, of course. What did you expect?"

She stuck her lip out in a dramatic pout. "Well I thought he said it was mine to keep."

He rolled his eyes. "You silly, silly girl. You have a lot to learn. Leprechauns are some of the most low-down, dishonest creatures I have ever met. Second only to horses of course."

"What do you have against horses?"

"What do I have against horses?" His voice rose. "*What do I have against horses?* My sister ran off with a horse and had a couple of hippogriffs. She had to move to Australia to save the family honor. My poor parents…"

Barnaby got up, shaking his head. "You had to go and ask him about horses. I'm going to go make us some tea. Heck, I might as well start dinner. He's going to be at this for hours."

Molly leaned back and closed her eyes, listening to the Griffin rant. She was home.

About the Author

Anne Harrington's sister once gave her some sound advice concerning writing: "Don't stop writing until you've finished the story." So Anne did. The first draft of "the Griffin's Feather" was written in 30 days as part of a NaNoWriMo Challenge. She realized then how much she loves to tell stories, and has been writing ever since. In addition Ms. Harrington is an artist, gardener and lover of all the unexpected magical things that can be found if you keep your eyes open and let your imagination wander.

Anne draws from her extensive knowledge of mythology, plant lore, art and magic to create a rich world of enchantment that will delight children and adults alike. "The Griffin's Feather" is the first in a series chronicling the adventures of Molly Stevens and her menagerie of magical friends.